The Sky Calls

2ND EDITION

by Hal Aetus

This is a work of fiction. Unless otherwise indicated, all the names, characters, businesses, places, events, incidents in this book are either the product of the author's imagination or used in a fictitious manner. Any resemblance to actual persons, living or dead, or actual events is purely coincidental.

THE SKY CALLS

Soft Cover ISBN-13: 979-8-9898252-1-9
Electronic Edition ISBN-13: 979-8-9898252-2-6

Published by:
Aetus Art
PO Box 44236
Milwaukee, Wisconsin, 53214, USA

Cover art and design by Hal Aetus

First Edition: December 2018 (Thurston Howl Publications)
Second Edition: March 2024 (Aetus Art)

Dedication

I DEDICATE THIS BOOK TO MY loving "eagle," my husband, Colin, who soars with me through life's thermals and downdrafts. Also to Buddy, a real eagle that first showed me what true love looks like, and taught me more about "eagle thought" than a mere human deserves.

Many thanks to Kyreeth, who commissioned the initial short story that inspired me to grow it into my first novel. It's people like them, through their encouragement and financial support, that make it possible for struggling new authors and artists to gain confidence and grow their craft.

I'm grateful to my primary editor for the first edition, Kaelan Rhywiol, for her helpful guidance, and to Thurston Howl Publishing who gave me my break into my first novel. Thank you to my friends and colleagues who encouraged me to write (and update) this book, and endured periods of silence while I stewed and created.

I also want to thank all the fans of transformation out there that inspired me to create more "tf" works since the first edition of The Sky Calls. And thank you to the wonderful readers who enjoyed the first edition enough to take time to communicate what it meant to them. For some it inspired interest in birds biology and anatomy. For others, it strengthened their innate yearnings to be a bird. But for everyone, it was a story of unshakable love in the face of adversity. I hope this new edition continues to inspire.

Chapter 1
A Good Guy

"I think over again my small adventures.
My fears, those small ones that seemed so big,
For all the vital things
I had to get and reach.
And yet there is only one great thing,
The only thing,
To live to see the great day that dawns
And the light that fills the world."
—Adaptation of a Kitlinermiut (Copper Inuit) song

DAVID GERAKI WAS A GOOD guy. To use the past tense like this may be misleading. He's not dead, and he didn't turn evil, but he isn't exactly a man anymore either. We need to roll back about two years to start unfolding this tale...

It began on a typical cool spring day in Seattle, Washington. The sky shone through in bright holes of blue between white, fluffy clouds, casting warm sunshine on the steamy, damp pavement. David left his apartment building West Seattle, biked down to the bus stop, arriving just in time to throw his bike on the rack and ride into town to go to work.

David worked at Everest Solutions, a software company, writing code for customized customer-management applications for retail clients. That might not sound exciting to you, but David had a sharp, organized mind that loved solving the puzzles inherent to being a software engineer. He was in his mid-thirties and had been married to his work for over twelve years, providing for his comfortable, but noticeably single, lifestyle.

David's day was routine, at first. He spent the morning at his cubicle, working away on debugging functions and procedures. Around eleven a.m. he received the fateful call. It was his doctor—not the physician's assistant. He had almost forgotten about his appointment a few days before. He had lost some weight and didn't have a great appetite, but he hoped that maybe he was just dodging the mid-life spare tire that his father had. He was overdue for a check-up anyway, so he had gone to see his general practitioner.

The voice on the phone was friendly: "This is Dr. Frank calling. How are you today?"

"I'm okay. No real change, and I still feel okay," David replied. "Good!" came Dr. Frank's reply. "Good. We found some values in your blood work that are higher than we like to see. They indicate some inflammation of your liver but we can't tell precisely why yet. We'd like to run some more tests on you including an ultrasound and potentially a biopsy. I'd like to have you come in as soon as possible for this."

David's world darkened and shrank around him. He stared down at his keyboard. "Is it serious?"

"I hate to guess on these sorts of things. The blood work just tips us off to a lot of different possible causes, some minor, some serious. Considering some of the more serious possibilities, it's best to explore it sooner than later. I'll transfer you up to the nurse and she can schedule your procedures for this week. Is that okay?"

"Sure . . . sure thing."

"Sorry if it seems alarming, but bear in mind that there's still plenty of benign reasons for elevated liver enzyme values. I'll be able to tell you a lot more after the tests. Do you have any more questions?"

"No, no. Thank you."

David scheduled his appointment and went back to working as best he could, but the rest of the day passed by in a haze of concern. A retirement party at the end of the day was a welcome distraction. The lucky retiree was Jim Truskie, one of Everest's founding engineers. He was 60 years old, had a wide nose, a full head of gray hair, and high cheekbones that complimented his frequent wide smile. Unlike other founders that had retired much earlier, Jim stuck around and stayed involved in the company.

As David arrived, Jim showed off pictures of a cherry red Porsche convertible that he had just purchased. It was excessive, flashy, and so unlike this humble man. A white-frosted cake, decorated with a log cabin and the words "Happy Retirement," rested on a table in the center of the break room. Coworkers added a novelty toy boat, an RV, and a sports car on it—all the things that Jim would be free to enjoy now.

David liked Jim as a boss and a trusted friend. He was amiable, generous, and sharp as a tack. He kept meetings short and ended on a positive note, even during unfortunate news. His humble confidence put David so much at ease that he often asked Jim for personal advice. Jim was the father figure that David never had.

Since the death of Jim's wife a few years earlier, David had seen a change in Jim's countenance. He was absent for much of his wife's last months of treatment, but returned to work immediately after her death. He said he was glad she was out of pain, but sometimes his eyes belied sadness and the need for work to distract him from the empty space her departure had created at home. Seeing him reminded David of aching loss, and at the same time, the rare sweetness of love that two people can have for each other. Jim was David's evidence that love both existed and was worth the pain. Its joys could be great enough to make it worth suffering through tremendous loss. He wanted to experience that joy. Work achievements and diversions with friends were not enough. He wanted a lifelong companion—someone to stir his heart clear to the end.

David had seen few examples of this kind of relationship in his lifetime. Certainly his parents were not the best role models for love, though he considered himself lucky to have had both of his parents and all the basic necessities growing up. They attended church on holidays, went on a family camping trip once a year, and put up reasonable appearances at least until he was a teenager. From the outside, they were an ideal family. But his parents didn't connect with him after the age of ten.

His dad grew emotionally distant from him and his mom when David was eleven. He wasn't angry or abusive, he just didn't express any emotion, even with his family. He would spend hours alone watching sports, smoking cigarettes, and drinking beer in the garage. He loved to hunt and fish and would be gone most weekends with buddies from work. In earlier years, he had tried to encourage David in these pursuits, but he sensed his son's hesitation. David was physically awkward and slight of build, so much so that a look of disappointment would cloud his dad's face whenever David tried to measure up to his manly expectations. David also asked a lot of questions, which gradually seemed like demands, and so finally he just left David at home.

David's mom worked night shifts as a nurse at the local hospital so that she could have time to herself during the day. Except for during the occasional visit with relatives, the small family rarely carried on conversations beyond the bare necessities of communication. David knew that he had pretty much raised himself and he felt that he'd managed pretty well.

At the party, Jim gave David a friendly hug. He put a firm hand on David's shoulder and said, "David, I see how you are, and I was a lot like you. You love your work maybe a bit too much. As your boss, I'm supposed to put the company first and encourage you to work more, and I've loved it. But you know you're more than an employee to me. Take my advice: take time to live. Find someone to share life with. Work will always be there but you never know when life will throw you a curve ball."

David studied Jim's eyes as he spoke and he saw the familiar mix of genuine concern and smoldering loss. He nodded his head. "I understand. Thanks for the advice. I'm gonna miss you . . . you've always been a good sounding board for me. I'm gonna stay in touch."

Jim smiled. "You bet! You'd better come to my cabin out in Colville for a few days. We'll forget all about this place and let you recharge."

David suddenly found himself wondering if he would be around that long. He caught himself, surprised at the prematurely morbid thought and forced a smile. "Sounds like fun. I'll take you up on that!"

Late that evening, David stood alone in his apartment looking out at Elliot Bay. Uncorking a bottle of whiskey, he sat down on the floor and leaned back against the wall. He skipped the formality of a glass, took a swig straight from the bottle, and looked out at the busy lights of the boats and the city. Drinking was probably the worst thing he could do for his liver. He didn't normally drink alone, but he had a lot to think about, and the alcohol helped temper the sting of realities swimming in his mind.

Bling! David's laptop chimed. He jerked awake and fumbled for it on the coffee table. He had been chatting online with his best friend, Sam, but his thoughts, and the alcohol, had slowed his responses. David had known Sam since they were prepubescent nerds in the ninth grade. They attended the same high school and roomed together in college at Washington State University. They were both into computers, but had taken different career paths.

While David delved into Information Technology, Sam

concentrated on a Bachelor's and a Master's degree in wildlife biology. He now worked for the Washington Department of Fish and Wildlife and lived in nearby Tacoma.

Neither of them had ever gotten hitched. They would get together on weekends sometimes and go for backpacking trips in the mountains or do a pub crawl in downtown Seattle. It was great fun, and David always looked forward to spending time with Sam.

Sam had sent several lines of chat messages a minute or so apart. They were about a game he had been playing, but this last one was 15 minutes after those and simply read, *You okay?*

David replied, *Not sure. Gotta go to doctor again tomorrow. Some shit about my liver.*

Thirty seconds later, Sam responded, *Serious?*

Not sure. maybe. drunk.. trying to forget bout it.

Sam responded immediately, *hope not serious. Need to have your liver for this weekend, bud. Still coming over for games and drinks, right? We'll kick some ass together.*

David typed back, *For sure. Gonna need it. CU Friday night. I'm gonna head to bed. Nini.*

Chapter 2
Sam

I T WASN'T SO BAD. THE technician was a nice guy. Kept talking to me the whole time," David said.

Sam chuckled. "Probably hitting on you."

He leaned back on his worn, supple, secondhand brown leather sofa. He was thicker in the shoulders and neck than David and stood an inch or two taller. His eyes were a shade darker than his brown hair and they currently sparkled from drinking beer. He wore an old, worn, white t-shirt with a tree on it that read "Biologists do it in the woods." He lived in a 1950s suburb in a typical single-level dwelling common in that neighborhood. There had been minor remodels throughout the years, but the house was nothing special. Between a dirt bike helmet, piles of stray clothing and junk mail, and cheaply framed nature prints on the walls, the living room had the clear signs of a bachelor with a busy life.

"Well, who wouldn't?" David took a swig of his beer while Sam chuckled.

"What did they do to ya anyway?"

"Ultrasound. They poked me with a giant-ass needle right here . . ." David pointed to his stomach.

"They have any idea what it is?" Sam frowned.

"Not yet. They asked about my drug use and sexual activities . . . which was pretty easy to answer."

"As in ZERO!"

"Pretty much. There was a couple of random encounters in college—I told you about that."

"Yeah, yeah, I think you made it up. But, hey, go on . . ."

"I guess hepatitis B can lead to cancer, and I've never been tested or vaccinated. So, of course, they sucked more blood for that."

There was silence for a moment, and then Sam said, "But, hey, there must be other, less serious causes. Otherwise they wouldn't bother testing, right? So when do ya find out?"

"Probably Monday." David replied as he peeled the label off his bottle of beer.

Sam put a warm hand on David's wrist and broke his introspection. "Hey, buddy. You be sure to call me when you get the news. We've been best buds for years. I'll be there for ya."

David appreciated the gesture and smiled back. "Thanks, man." He inhaled and blew out loudly. "It's gotten morbid in here . . . I think you're just stalling on that rematch!"

They went on to spend the evening drinking and playing video games into the wee hours of the morning. David eventually found himself lying on the couch, the room spinning around him. He looked over to see Sam sprawled back on some pillows on the floor, lightly snoring while the movie they'd been watching continued to play.

One of Sam's shirts was under the back of David's head and he realized, for the first time, he liked the smell of it. He always had. It didn't arouse him, but it surrounded him with a familiar and unbiased favor. He loved the feeling, the reminder, that someone gave a shit about him. It was worth more to him than any brief rapture sex could provide. He stared at the ceiling and contemplated their friendship.

Despite going different directions in life and all the different people they had studied and worked with, neither Sam nor David had ever found other friends with whom they were more comfortable. They could have been married for how well they knew each other.

Both of them had been different from their schoolmates. In Enumclaw, Washington in the 1990s, there wasn't much social opportunity for computer and science nerds but their awkwardness went beyond just that. They didn't share the same interests as their classmates, particularly when it came to traditional gender roles or relationships. Sam was better at feigning interest in girls than David but with the exception of fulfilling the expectations of his family by taking a girl to the prom, Sam never really dated or pursued girls.

David had no interest in girls at all and, as a teenager, had kept to himself or spent time with Sam. While hormone-soaked young men around him rolled their tongues about the physical attributes of girls in their classes, he would give simple, well-conditioned responses that agreed with them. Women did not arouse him and he was careful to avoid the question, even within himself, of whether men aroused him instead. He was uncertain, and it was very confusing that he didn't share the interests of other young men. But he knew that if he didn't respond naturally to heteronormative banter, he would become the butt of his classmates' jokes. It wasn't until the liberal environment of college, where he could see that being homosexual was acceptable, that he fully admitted to himself he was gay. Once he accepted that reality inside, he admitted it externally to others.

Sam had likewise come to terms with his sexual orientation in college. Sam's parents were proud of him regardless and his mother joked that she knew about it long before Sam's confession. But his parents were far more liberal than average for rural Washington at that time.

As David fuzzily recollected his history with Sam he marveled at how, despite their common backgrounds and interests and the incredible friendship they had, they had never become more than friends. Neither of them surprised the other when they came out of the closet; they had shared plenty about their secret confusion over heterosexual expectations. It had always been enough to be friends and build incredible memories together.

Alcohol clouds the senses but sometimes sharpens reality. Sometimes it lowers our internal defenses enough that we see truths about ourselves we've avoided. And so it was, David learned that the simple smell of Sam's shirt comforted him. He realized that he could totally fall for Sam if he allowed it to happen. The advice that Jim had given him reverberated in his throbbing brain and he reached out a hand and softly petted Sam's head.

David slurred softly, "Thanks, Sam. You're the best."

Sam gave a soft sigh and shifted his body in response.

David spent the night on the couch, waking up now and then to a dull ache in his midsection that reminded him of where the doc had stabbed him. Each time he remembered he also wondered if his life would ever go back to the way it had been and then he would reach out and touch his friend for reassurance. As dawn came, and he repeated this routine for the fourth or fifth time, he considered whether he really wanted his life to carry on as it had been—solitary. *No*, he thought to himself, *I'm done being in this rut. One way or the other, things are going to be different.*

Chapter 3
The Worst News Ever

AVID TOOK THE AFTERNOON OFF after he received the call from the doctor. The doc simply asked him to come down to discuss results in person. He had no appetite for breakfast or lunch that day but, then again, he was anxious. Still, he had been nervous before without losing his appetite, so he was pretty sure it was more than nerves that stole his appetite.

He waited only five minutes in the doctor's office but for once he didn't mind. He dreaded the news he might receive, and he wanted to just stay in the bliss of pretending everything was going to be okay. When a nurse came and fetched him, he felt his heart sink like a stone. He couldn't pretend any more. Either he'd be leaving elated or his world was coming to an end. He didn't think it would be anything in between.

She showed him to a consultation room, closed the door, and logged in to a computer. David's mind drifted for a moment as he noticed the software interface and some quirks about it. He couldn't help but see improvements that he could make if it was his product. He smirked at himself, realizing that this was hardly the time to be thinking about work with his life hanging in the balance. The nurse asked a few questions, and then Dr. Frank entered.

Dr. Frank was a white man in his fifties with a soft bulge around his middle and narrow, soft facial features. He had brown hair, mixed with hints of gray, and silver, bushy brows above his gray-green eyes. Another doctor was with him, both wearing the white coats of the profession.

Dr. Frank greeted David and shook his hand as they closed the door behind them. "The biopsy came back conclusive. You have hepatic carcinoma . . . cancer, I'm afraid. I've asked Dr. Morgan to come in since he's an oncologist and can help us work out your treatment."

Dr. Morgan, a short, dark-complexioned man, stepped forward. He had dark hair and dark eyes that looked out through tiny, round glasses under thick eyebrows. He had some gray showing in his hair and he bore a serious but warm look on his soft, fleshy cheeks. "I'm sorry to meet you this way, Mr. Geraki." He reached out and shook David's stunned hand.

"Yeah, me too. Liver cancer, eh?" David replied

"Yes, I'm afraid so," Dr. Morgan said. "We can't stage it yet without doing some more imaging, but the biopsy confirms it's there. Your Hepatitis B test came back positive as well. You had mentioned some unprotected sex fifteen years ago. It's likely that's when you were infected. The virus can lie dormant and never cause problems. In others it will cause hepatitis, and in a small percentage of people it can lead to cancer."

Dr. Morgan went on to describe how the cancer would be "staged," a process of determining the severity and spread, and he laid out the initial treatment options. Since cancer is a very serious disease, David was advised to "get his affairs in order" while he was still relatively healthy and fully able to do so.

Despite the heavy news, though, Dr. Morgan somehow conveyed an attitude of hope. He worked with Tukwila Cancer Center, a large research hospital well-known for its cutting-edge advances with many types of cancers.

David drove home slowly after his appointment. When he was all alone at home in his empty condo, the reality finally sank in. He opened the drapes of the glass balcony door and looked out at the blue waters and cloud-flecked sky. Cars, boats, planes, people, birds . . . all going about their usual lives.

Inside himself, David felt a heavy surge of gravity, like concrete forming in the pit of his stomach, pulling him down to the floor as he sobbed. He cried until the sun angled lower and warmed his shoulders. Then he remembered his promise to call Sam. He pulled out his cell phone and found that there were already three missed calls and a message. His heart warmed, and he smiled.

I forgot I silenced it! He sat up, wiped his eyes with his hand, and pressed the button to call Sam back.

Sam answered immediately. "Hey, buddy, how's it going?"

David swallowed hard and then spoke with a shaky voice. "Not so good . . . goddamn cancer."

David expected Sam to go silent and search for the right words to say. Instead, he responded immediately and calmly, "It's going to be okay, buddy. You'll be all right. I'll be right there with you every step of the way. I'm gonna knock off work and come over there, okay?"

David lost track of his own concern for just a moment as he realized how certain his friend sounded. His calmness and certitude comforted him like a warm, strong hand on the back of his neck. Normally he might resist putting someone through such trouble but Sam's voice told him that it wouldn't matter if he objected. Besides, he really did need Sam's level head right now. "Sure, Sam, I'd like that. I'll see ya soon."

When Sam knocked at the door, David woke up. He had fallen asleep in the same spot by the glass door. The sun was setting, and the street lights cast an orange glow on the avenue below. He stroked his face, griddled and stinging from being pressed against the carpet. He wiped his eyes with the sleeve of his shirt and fumbled for something to blow his nose. Pushing through the fog of drained emotions, he gradually realized that he was at home and Sam was at the door.

There was another rapid knock and a muffled, "David? Are you okay?"

David cleared his throat as he slowly rose to his feet. "I'm coming, Sam!"

As David let him in, Sam could see by the swollen, red eyes what had happened. Sam had a bag of hot chicken in one hand and a six-pack in the other. He set them down on the floor and reached his arms around to hug David close. David embraced Sam back and absorbed the warm comfort that he had experienced when sleeping on Sam's shirt a few days before. For the fleeting moment, things seemed okay.

David whispered, "Thanks for coming over."

Sam hugged tighter and rocked him a little. "You bet. Have you eaten yet? I brought us some dinner."

David realized he hadn't eaten all day. His appetite hadn't been normal, but right now, that chicken smelled amazing. They ate and had a beer together while David told Sam all about what the doctors had said and he listened attentively.

At one point, when David had relaxed enough, he found himself staring down at his beer bottle saying, "I'm actually pretty lucky."

Sam gave an exaggerated eyebrow raise. "Lucky?!"

"No, no . . . not lucky I have cancer. I'm lucky because at least I have insurance that should take care of this, I have some money put away, I live where I can get excellent care, and, most of all, I have a good friend like you around to make it seem okay."

Sam shifted around a little in his chair and David looked up at him. A bit of moisture in the corners of his eyes, Sam replied, "You're my best friend, David. I know you'd do the same for me. I'm probably gonna drive you crazy checking in all the time. Be sure to let me know when your appointments are, and I'll be there with ya. And we're gonna have to go do some of those special hikes we've been putting off for forever."

David thought about that a moment then snickered. "Shit. Remember that time I made you promise to go skydiving with me?"

Sam's face went blank. "No. I don't know what you're talking about."

David gave him a shove. "Fuck you! You were stone sober at the time so I know you remember it."

Sam laughed and rolled his eyes. "Yeah, yeah, dammit I'm gonna regret it now!"

"Well, yeah, I know that you're not wild about it. But I was thinking today, I've always wanted to hang glide. It seems a lot like being a bird. Maybe instead of skydiving you'd want to go hang gliding with me? There's a place in Issaquah that does lessons."

Sam cocked his head and took a drink of beer. "Yeah, I gotta admit, whenever I see birds of prey soaring around, I wonder what it's like. Sounds a lot more appealing than just falling like bird shit from the sky." After a moment of looking up in thought he nodded his head and said, "Okay, you're on!"

Chapter 4
Excision

THAT WEEK DAVID UNDERWENT MORE tests. MRI scans, more blood work, and an upper GI endoscopy. By the end of the week, the doctors had enough information to label David's prognosis as "grave." It was an appropriately gloomy term to him. He felt that he would soon be in a grave, so why not call it for what it really was. In addition to his liver, there was a mass in his right lung. He was a hapless tree caught in a landslide, hurtling down toward oblivion, and all he felt he could do was watch it happen—watch his body crumble and crash down.

The details of his treatment were largely beyond his control. Sure, the doctors presented choices, but could he really refuse their advice? He had no better plans, and the urgency of his condition meant he couldn't waste much time seeking other opinions. Barely ten days after his diagnosis, and that fateful meeting with his doctors, he underwent surgery to remove as much of the cancer as possible and prepare him for further treatment. The hope was that surgery would buy the time he needed to explore all of his remaining options.

After surgery, Sam waited by David's hospital bed in the recovery room, waiting for him to gain consciousness.

"Hey…" David whispered, blinking his red, squinty eyes.
Sam looked up with surprise and leaned forward. He

said gently, "Hey, man. How are ya?"

"Been better."

"Yeah, no shit," Sam said. He grabbed a cup of ice and offered some on a spoon. "Not too tasty but they said it would be helpful to offer ya when you woke up." David opened his mouth and took a couple of the ice chips.

David looked down his front and saw the tubes coming out from under his gown and the blanket across his middle. His arms were lightly bound down. They'd told him that might be the case but it was still scary. He passed it off with a wisecrack: "How do I . . . look in bondage? Now's . . . your chance . . . to take advantage . . . of me."

Sam snickered. "Who says I haven't already?" David laughed weakly. "Damn, that . . . hurts!"

Sam put a hand on David's left arm. "You want me to get the nurse and have 'em pump more feel-goods into ya?"

"No, no . . . I'm okay. Have . . . you seen . . . the doc . . . yet?" Just then a female nurse entered and interrupted them. "Ah! I saw your vitals speed up on the monitor. Glad to see you're awake." She leaned over and shined a light in David's eyes, checked his tubes and the IV pumps. "Dr. Morgan will be in soon and go over everything." She made David wiggle his toes, raised the head of his bed a little, plumped up his pillows,

and made sure he was comfortable.

By the time she had finished, Dr. Morgan came into the room. He greeted Sam with a smile. "Hi there, Sam. How's our patient?"

"He's awake and I can see you didn't remove his sense of humor."

Dr. Morgan turned to David. "Oh? Well that's good to hear. How are you feeling?"

"Alright . . . considering," David said between short breaths. "It's a little harder to breathe . . . and I see the tube . . . in my chest . . . I guess . . . you took part . . . of a lung?" "That's right," Dr. Morgan said. "About twenty-five percent of your right lung, and we also had to remove about thirty percent of your liver. As we suspected, your cancer is stage Four-B since it has spread to other organs. You still have a decent amount of functional liver tissue remaining, though, so we have a bit of time to let you heal up before we begin other therapies."

David exhaled with a little catch in his breath as he winced from a sharp pain stabbing his lower chest. "So that'll be . . . radiation?"

Dr. Morgan sat on a stool and rolled closer to David. "Possibly. But there's also a brand new experimental therapy that involves gene editing. I know you're a smart guy and you've been doing some online research. You may have heard of the CRISPR-Cas9 system, which has been in the news lately."

David perked up a little, "Yes . . . I did . . . Go on . . ."

Dr. Morgan nodded. "It's been a great tool for editing genomes in specific tissues, such as tumors. Then there's also TALEN, which is a fancy acronym for a process using enzymes that cut DNA at specific spots. The two techniques can be combined with powerful results. We can also modulate the gene editing using 'safe genes' to switch the process on and off. It's new, but shows great promise and I think you should consider it. We expect it will, at the very least, buy you some additional time and quality of life, but there's even a possibility it could cure you."

David nodded sleepily. "I'm . . . game. Do what you need . . . to do."

"I don't want to get your hopes up too high, because it's such a new therapy you would be one of only 3 people that have tried it. But trials in animals have been simply astonishing."

David's eyelids sank. He yanked them up slightly. "Uh-huh . . ." He faded back into sleep as the doctor said something about discussing it further at a later time.

Over the next few days, despite the sharp pain in his chest and side, David gained energy, his appetite returned, and he felt better. After a week in the hospital, David anxiously waited to leave and try to live as normally as possible again. Sam picked him up, and on the drive to David's house, they talked about the treatments to come.

Sam stopped his small, white pickup truck at a traffic light and asked David, "Are you having nurses come over?"

David rubbed his right side. "Yeah. This nurse will come by once a day to check on me for a while. I have to come back here in a week if things are going well."

After some silence the light changed and they drove on. Sam asked, "What do you think of the gene editing therapy the doc talked about?"

"I've been reading up on it. Of course what I find on the internet is pretty vague since the Cancer Center's trials are still unfinished and unpublished. I'd essentially be their guinea pig. But, hell, what do I have to lose since I'm gonna die from this anyway."

Sam glanced at David then back to the road. "I don't know how you can say it so plainly like that. Shit, I'd still be in denial if I was you. I can barely accept it. How do you take it so well?"

David looked down at the sore spot on his arm where a catheter had been, and rubbed it. "I started working through this before I knew it was cancer. I was already sick of my complacency about life. Cancer just give me a more tangible target to get pissed at and then depressed about. But I really want to live, now more than ever. I figure the best way to fight for life is to realize that I'm probably going to die very soon."

Sam reached over and took David's hand and squeezed it. "Hopefully not too soon, you bastard. We still have things to do together . . . including those gliders to hang from." That got the desired chuckle from David. "Seriously, though.

You're my hero right now. Cancer and death are fucking scary things to me, and you're making them seem . . . more like bad guys that need to be put down with a head shot."

"You're pretty much my hero right now too. I couldn't face this so well if it wasn't for your support. Thank you, Sam."

David spent a welcome week at home enjoying daily walks and nightly meals with Sam. But the break came to an end and soon he was back at the hospital undergoing more scans and tests. More masses were arising in his liver, much sooner than expected. Within a few days his condition began to slide downhill. He lost his appetite again, and despite making himself eat, his weight dropped.

Dr. Morgan brought in another research associate to speak with David about the experimental gene therapy. He would have to live at the hospital for at least a few weeks. If it worked, he could expect improvement within a week. If it didn't that would be clear pretty quickly, too.

Dr. Dennis Dunmeier, the head research oncologist, was a tall, gaunt, middle-aged black man with a chiseled, clean-shaven face and well-groomed black hair edged with gray around his temples. His eyes had a clarity and shape that demanded your attention, like a stare from a hawk. He explained the treatment with a calm, clear voice.

"Here's how it works, David. We use tissue cultures, created from tumors that were removed during your surgery, to optimize plasmids that will deliver nucleases directly to the DNA of cancer cells. Nucleases are molecules that will cut the DNA of just those cells, replace the viral and other damaged DNA, and allow normal repair mechanisms to finish the job. Those cells will then produce more of the nucleases to treat neighboring cells.

"For safety, we will also prepare treatments that can specifically interrupt this process so that we can control it, should there be any adverse effects we haven't accounted for.

Other than some soreness and mild-to-moderate fever and feelings of illness, which would probably be less than you're experiencing presently, it should not affect your quality of life significantly.

"But we need to keep you here as this treatment is new, and we need to track every bit of your progress. Also, any body fluids have to be collected, analyzed, and disposed of specially since you are taking unproven biologically-active drugs."

David felt buoyed by the doctor's optimism. "I'm interested. The sorafenib is obviously not helping. What about radiation and chemo?"

Dr. Dunmeier continued, "You would have to forego more conventional therapies like chemo or radiation, at least at first. This is risky but, as you are already aware, these treatments do not offer a great increase in survival for your type of cancer. And, because of their direct effects on healing tissues, we would have to let you heal for a couple more weeks before we could use them anyway. But we can start this treatment tomorrow if you like."

David sat up straight in his chair. "Tomorrow?"

Dr. Dunmeier nodded. "Yep. We've already grown the tissue cultures and run some tests. Your cancer shows excellent compatibility with the treatment. We could finish preparing your protocol by tomorrow morning. We could set you up in one of our treatment suites upstairs today, and run a few remaining tests, so you're all set to go first thing in the morning." David nodded and rubbed his right side with a wince.

"Okay, where do I sign?"

Dr. Morgan looked over at Sam then back at David. "Are you sure about this? You fellas can take a little time to discuss this in private if you want."

Sam tilted his forehead with lifted eyebrows. "I can go back to your place and get your things. It's your call, buddy."

"No, no . . . there's no question about it. I've thought of nothing but this damn cancer for weeks now. I've read up a bit on this therapy. I know that it's cutting edge and might not work. I could get a second opinion, but I don't think that I have a lot of time to mess around. From the sound of it, what do I have to lose?"

So, David signed the release forms and had Sam bring him some of his things from home. By the end of the day, he sat in his hospital bed in the research suite, eating his last meal before fasting for the first treatment in the morning. Sam joined him for dinner.

"Sorry, no beer this time," Sam said as he sipped a glass of water. "But I'm in this with ya, so none for me either."

"Aw, Sam, you can have one if you want. I can barely eat, so beer doesn't sound all that great anyway." David picked at his institutional whipped potatoes with fat-free gravy. He set down his plastic fork and pushed it away.

"Are ya scared?"

"Not really. Hell, this is the least scary thing to happen through this whole crap show. I'm anxious to get it going and see what happens. If it works . . . well, everything will be different in my life. I'm not going to just work and ignore relationships any more. I don't want to be alone." He looked up at Sam. "But I don't know if I dare hope that much."

Sam grasped his hand and smiled, "Hey, bud. We're both daring to hope that much."

Sam stayed with David late into the evening, and they chatted about their experiences together. Sam had to bring up the time that David and he were on a hike in eastern Washington and went skinny dipping in a wilderness creek. Suddenly they realized they were surrounded by a squad of ROTC cadets practicing their stealth and survival skills. Sam had just smiled up at one of the camouflaged figures and said, "Hey, the water's great! Come on in!" They'd told these stories a thousand times, but they never failed to still get them chuckling.

After Sam had left and David was unsuccessfully at-
tempting to sleep, he re-evaluated his attitude of not having
lived his life fully enough. He'd experienced some pretty cool
things. After all, how many people ever dare to go skinny dipping in the wilderness? Remembering his experiences and
the friend he shared them with helped him finally sink into
peaceful sleep.

Chapter 5
Infusion

THE NEXT MORNING, A NEW IV bag hung next to David's bed. It bore a large, bright orange sticker that read "Experimental Protocol 221." A biohazard sign on his door indicated that everyone should wear masks. As they turned on the IV pump, and he saw the clear fluid enter his vein, he sighed and wonder what would happen next. No head rush, no strange sensations, nothing new happened. He napped, watched TV, and poked around the Internet on his laptop, dreaming of the things he would do when he left the hospital. Before he knew it, the sun sank low over the jagged blue peaks of the Olympic Mountains, and a warm, orange glow splashed the wall in front of his bed. That's when Sam showed up for a visit.

"Hey wingman," Sam said as he warmly clasped David's hand between his own. He asked the cliché question, "Feel any different yet?"

David snickered. "No, and I suppose that's a good thing, right? They said that it'll take . . . a while . . ." David clenched his eyes and rubbed them with his fingers.

Sam leaned forward with his brows wrinkled in concern. "You sure you're okay?"

David opened his eyes again and blinked them. "Yeah, I think so. It's just that things look a little weird. Like colors are super bright, and the sunshine on the wall there looks psychedelic." He shook his head with an oddly quick twitch, but the saturated colors were still there.

Sam nodded at the door. "Want me to get someone?"

"No, not yet. I want to talk a bit first. It doesn't hurt or anything. Probably just from looking at my laptop too much. How was your day?"

Sam sat down in a chair by the bed. "Pretty awesome. Looks like I'll be helping with bald eagle management stuff for a little while. Their population is so strong now that we have to overhaul regulations for landowners with nests on their property. And we have to figure out how to mediate damage to heron rookeries and nesting ospreys. It's gonna be a lot of public meetings, Jerry Springer style . . ." Sam stopped as he saw David scratch his head and come back with a clump of his dark hair in his fingers. "Looks like I'm gonna have to start knitting you one of those cancer hats. I sucked in Home Ec, so it'll look like crap."

David looked at the hair with astonishment. "That's weird. It's not supposed to do that. Maybe I'd better talk to the doctor." He pressed his nurse call button, and she soon came in. Minutes later, Dr. Dunmeier and a research resident were taking a look at David. They ordered some blood work and stepped out of the room for a few minutes while a nurse sat nearby. Sam stayed with David, watching his breathing pick up pace.

"David, it's gonna be okay. Stay with me buddy." Sam tried to remain calm and keep David focused on him instead of panicking. David's eyes flicked about nervously and his fingers twitched. An alarm sounded on David's heart monitor and the readout escalated dramatically. 100, 120, 150, 180, then 200 beats per minute. David's eyes rolled back and his arms and legs shuddered.

Sam helped the nurse grab David's flailing arms. She looked toward the door and shouted out "Doctor! Seizure!"

The doctors shot back in and started shouting orders while nurses held David's arms and legs and pushed injections into his IV line. Sam backed up but kept his eyes on David's between the wall of white coats and green scrubs that crowded about until someone finally asked him to leave.

Minutes later, they wheeled David down the hallway to the Intensive Care Unit. Sam followed until they plunged through windowed doors that read "Staff Only." He stood there as the doors closed, watching his friend disappear down a white corridor. He felt the chilly edge of finality, as though the sterile doors slapping shut in his face meant that he would never see David alive again.

Hours later, he awoke in a waiting room chair. Dr. Dunmeier was looking down at him, saying, "Sam?"

Sam sat up slowly, rubbing the kink in his neck as his cell phone slid off of his lap and clattered to the floor. He glanced around while he picked it up and saw that the time was almost one a.m.

"Oh man, I fell asleep. How's David? Can I see him?"

"David's okay for the moment."

Dr. Dunmeier sat down next to Sam, "You can't see him yet. Not tonight. David signed consent forms for you to have power of attorney, right?"

Sam swallowed and replied, "Yeah, that's right. His mom died a few years back and his dad's been out of things for years. No other immediate family."

Dr. Dunmeier removed his glasses and massaged his tired eyes. "Well it would appear that there's been a speed bump with David's treatment. It's changing his physiology more than we expected, impacting systems—most obviously his central nervous system—outside of where the cancer exists. It's possible that there are early tumors in his brain that have formed since our last sets of scans. So far he's responding to standard therapies to control the symptoms, but he's not out of the woods yet."

"What about his eyesight and his hair falling out?" Sam asked.

The doctor shifted in his seat, like he had sat on a pebble. Sam could tell that the doctor wished he hadn't asked that question.

"Well, I'm not sure yet. I haven't seen anything like this in our other human patients. Tomorrow, I'll check with the animal trials team, which are at another facility that's closed at the moment."

Sam looked the doctor's face over, searching for more answers, but he didn't see any. "Well, okay. Thanks, doc. I'm glad he's hanging in there. Let me know when you have more."

"I suggest you go home, get some sleep. We have him on sedatives, so he'll be sleeping soundly until mid-morning. We'll take excellent care of him. I suggest checking back around 9 or so."

Dr. Dunmeier stood up and watched as Sam left the lobby. He rubbed his head, turned and walked back down the corridor to his office. He closed the door, took off his white coat and dropped it on a chair stacked with medical journals, and sat down at his desk. He picked up an empty vial sealed in a doubled biohazard bag. The label on the bag read "Human Protocol #221, Subject: Geraki, David."

"Shit!" he cursed quietly as he shook his head slowly. He propped his elbows on the desk and rested his forehead in his hands. He slowly shook his head and muttered, "How the hell did this happen? How in the living hell . . . ?"

He set the package down on the desk and on the side of the vial, inside the bag, in near-illegible handwriting it read, "Experimental Protocol #221, Subject: 002 Golden Eagle."

Chapter 6
State of Flux

WARMTH SPILLED OVER DAVID'S FACE, and dark red light filtered through his closed eyelids. When he opened them, he stood on the brim of a wide, rocky canyon. Tall, dark-gray basalt columns marched along the walls of the canyon, giving way to short rocky slopes of broken, stony polygons at their bases. Below this rolled tall, yellow grass, green sage brush, and a thin row of shimmering poplar and willow along the edges of a broad, blue river far below. David looked up, and above the cliffs he saw a golden plateau rolling into the distance and snow-laced blue-gray peaks on the horizon. David blinked his eyes hard and cocked his head at the brilliant lavender glow he perceived in the distant mountain snow.

The location was familiar, as though he were at a scenic overlook along the Columbia River in Central Washington. But no freeway cut the hills, no wind turbines dotted the landscape, and no highway noise pierced his hearing. And he had no recollection of how he'd gotten there.

David marveled at the bright colors. Familiar white flowers vibrated with light purplish auras. Lichens popped with glowing orange and green. Among the grasses below, he could perceive fluorescent yellow patches and dark trodden game trails. He could actually count the leaves on the sagebrush far across the canyon, a mile away. He rubbed his eyes with his hand, but the hallucination continued. When he looked down the cliffs to the water, he saw tiny ripples stirred by the wind, and hungry fish darting in and out of the shadows. Sparrows darted and rabbits browsed in the grass along the banks. He shook his head in wonderment at the clarity.

Then he noticed Sam up the river on the near bank under a bending willow tree with a fishing pole and a line in the water. Suddenly, his pole jerked and bent low. He hooted out and fought to reel in a fish.

David yelled out, "Way to go!" and without hesitation he leapt off cliff like nothing could be more natural. He spread his arms and glided down faster and faster, the wind rushing in his ears. He landed easily on the grass near Sam, and cheered him on as he pulled a fat, shiny salmon from the river. Its scales flashed and sparkled iridescent hues that were near-holographic.

David rubbed his eyes yet again to try to clear them, and when he looked, the hospital was nearby, just beyond the willow trees up the bank of the river.

Sam asked with a worried look, "Are you okay? Maybe we better go back?"

David looked down at himself and realized that he wore a blue hospital gown with no back. He suddenly felt naked and out of place. "I feel fine but where's my clothes?"

Sam just said, "David, come on, let's go back."

In just a few steps, David found himself back in his room. Two doctors and a nurse were conversing with each other while Sam excitedly re-enacted for David how he had caught the salmon. The surroundings were familiar, and yet completely unhinging. The walls were too close and the crowd was too loud.

David yelled out in a stifled, raspy voice, "Stop! Stop! It's too goddamn noisy in here!" but nobody heard him. The nurses banged things around, and Sam just kept telling his fish story. David shouted louder, "Sam! Listen to me! Shut up for a minute and kick everyone outta here!" Despite yelling harder his voice grew no louder. His throat felt obstructed and nobody could hear him. They just kept doing their own things, completely oblivious to his struggle. David gasped and choked, his throat tightening with panic. He tried to reach for his mouth but his arms were tightly strapped down. His eyebrows broke in sweat and his heart raced. "What . . . the . . . hell?!" he croaked out in a gravelly whisper. The room went blurry and dark as he struggled to breath and then he heard beeping that grew louder and louder . . .

A firm hand shook his shoulder, and a young woman's voice shouted, "David! It's just a dream! Wake up!" As he opened his eyes, monitors beeped insistently. A slender, brunette nurse with long, tied-back hair leaned over him. David had not seen her before. He jolted awake in his hospital bed but couldn't move his arms or sit up. There was a tube in his throat, and he couldn't speak. His eyes widened, and he breathed deeper and faster.

"David! It's okay, you're all right. You had some unexpected reactions to the treatment, so we've put in a breathing tube." The nurse looked steadily into his eyes. "You're okay, breathe normally."

David gradually realized that he had been dreaming and that he was, indeed, able to breathe fine despite having an object lodged in his larynx. He relaxed and his breathing slowed down. The alarms stopped, and his eyes darted around the unfamiliar room.

"That's it. Good," came the calming nurse's voice. "You're going to be fine."

She took David's left hand in hers and she gave a polite squeeze. "I'm April, your nurse for this shift. You're in the ICU, and you're doing great. I'll let Dr. Dunmeier know that you're awake now. Do you want me to raise your head?"

David nodded and blinked his eyes. The nurse smiled with the most amazing thin, red lips. Her blue uniform had the same, surreal purplish glow that he had seen in his dream. He fluttered his eyelids in a way that felt peculiar. It did the job, but it felt like he blinked without closing his eyes. The nurse's smile faltered slightly and her eyes widened as if she were struggling to maintain a confident demeanor. She fumbled with the controls for the hospital bed, and then smiled and raised David's head up so that he could see the rest of the room. He tried to speak but the breathing tube gave him a sharp ache and he started to cough.

April urged him, "Don't try to speak! Now that you're breathing on your own, we'll probably take that out in a little bit." She pushed an injection into a port on David's IV lines and then set herself to checking other things in and around David's bed.

David's senses dulled, and he sank back into the pillows. His eyes narrowed and the world became fuzzy and warm. His dreamy world began to saturate his consciousness to the point that he couldn't quite tell dream from reality. If he opened his eyes, the world poured in with details, motion, and colors he had never noticed before. When he closed them he saw ghostly purple explosions, blue sparkles, and yellow swirls. He wondered when he would wake from his drug-enhanced dreams, and he quietly hoped that maybe everything had been a dream, including the cancer. If so, maybe he would wake up at home in bed, healthy and whole again.

Despite his sensory perturbations, David's chest and belly felt lighter and the stiff, grating fullness he'd been experiencing for weeks had nearly disappeared. The pain in his side was also gone. Perhaps things were going well after all.

Hours later, Dr. Dunmeier came in. His short curly hair looked disheveled, and his eyes were bloodshot. He looked like he had just woken up and washed his face in a drinking fountain. He smiled, and said in a gravelly voice, "Good morning, David." He wheeled up close to David on a stool and began studying his face and feeling his body over. "You gave us a little excitement overnight. Does this hurt?" he asked as he gently prodded David's upper abdomen. David slowly shook his head.

After a few more minutes of physical exam the doctor scribbled some notes and then wheeled up a little closer to David's right side. "So, let me update you, David. You're doing very well but something extraordinary has happened."

David cocked his head in a peculiar way to listen, and the doctor paused a moment while putting his pen in the waist pocket of his white coat.

He continued, "Well, this treatment is being studied in a number of animal models at an off-site research facility, which is also where the laboratory that processes human tissue samples and replicates the necessary primers and other products that went into your treatment is located. There seems to have been . . . well, a little confusion in processing orders. Don't worry, your treatment is going well. It's just going to happen a little differently than planned."

David furrowed his eyebrows in confusion.

Dr. Dunmeier placed his hands in his lab coat pockets and fidgeted with a pen. "Like I said, David, you seem to be responding to treatment. I don't anticipate any serious danger to your health but I don't know what all the side effects are going to be. Since your condition has stabilized, we'll run some new scans today and have more information for you. In the meantime, try to relax and we'll have that breathing tube out in a few minutes."

The doctor tapped a button on an IV pump, and David's eyelids grew heavier. His mind buzzed with questions, but he had no way to ask them. He was strong, warm, and full of potential but a heavy blanket of sleepiness weighed him down. He remembered naps as a young boy. He would want to crawl around and explore to no end, but sleepiness would overtake him until he couldn't keep his eyes open. His body would take over and force him to rest, repair, and grow.

He lingered on that image of himself as a young boy falling asleep in a sunny spot on the living room rug. He felt safe and content as he drifted into deep sleep again.

As David sank out of consciousness, April returned and helped Dr. Dunmeier remove the breathing tube. She noticed Dr. Dunmeier's hands shaking and saw his wide-eyed expression as he peered into David's throat with the laryngoscope. What she couldn't see was that David's throat had changed.

Humans normally have a covering called the epiglottis over their tracheal opening. David's was gone. There was also a cleft in the roof of his mouth, and his tongue was narrowing and stiffening. As Dr. Dunmeier withdrew the laryngoscope, one of David's lower incisors came with it.

April's eyes fastened to the bloody tooth. "What the—?"

Dr. Dunmeier cleared his throat. "It's okay, April, it's okay, I thought that this might happen soon. Let's get him ready to go down to radiology for an MRI."

April checked and secured David's various catheters and tubes. When she came to his urinary collection bag she stopped. She was a professional and not given to melodramatic impulses, but she'd never seen anything like this.

"Dr. Dunmeier!" she cried. "What . . . is this?"

She held the bag so that the doctor could see a semi-viscous goo of yellow and white. He looked at her with worried eyes. "Thanks, April. Make note of it."

She questioned him further, "But what is this? Is he dehydrated? He's received all of his prescribed fluids. Should we submit some to the lab for analysis?"

Dr. Dunmeier looked at her, then the bag, then at her, rocking back on his heels, trying to think of how to handle this. He couldn't conceal the truth much longer, but he didn't know how he was going to spin the mistake yet either. He could see that she knew that he was in over his head.

Dr. Dunmeier said firmly, "There's more going on here

but I don't have time to go into detail right now. Yes, please take a sample for the lab. Meanwhile, I really need to get some more imaging done, pronto."

Chapter 7
Quality of Life

SAM'S CHEEK WAS SWEATY FROM holding his cellphone against it for so long. He was through being nice.

"Look, lady, I've been told that same thing for three days now! You keep telling me to come back later. I know that I'm not family, but David signed a form that gave me power of attorney and rights to visit. If there's something wrong, I have a legal right to know. If you don't let me visit then I'm going to the police!"

There was a pause on the other end. *Sorry for the misunderstanding, sir. The doctor would like a conference with you today. When can you come down?*

Sam grabbed his keys and stood up, "I'm on my way right now, and he'd better be ready to talk!"

The nurse started to say something back, but Sam pressed End and cut her off.

Minutes later he sped onto Interstate 5 on his way to the hospital. He stared intensely down the road and weaved around slower cars.

"Fucking assholes. What the hell did they do to him? He could be dying for all I know, and they don't give a flying fuck except to cover their own ass!"

Sam screeched his tires as he swerved into the hospital parking lot. He walked right past the check-in desk, and went straight to the cancer research ward's ICU. He'd exerted a lot of energy on his way in, but still fumed. He tried to compose himself as he approached the nurse's station at a fast walk. "I'm Sam Grand, here to see David Geraki . . . where is he?"

The duty nurse said, "Dr. Dunmeier is coming right now, wait just a moment."

"No, no, no . . . I want to see David. NOW! And you have no legal right to stop me!" He moved away from the desk and started darting his head around at the ICU bays. He didn't see David's name or catch any familiar glimpses of his friend, so he strode toward the first room.

The nurse called after him, "Sir! Please stop! He's in room five!"

Sam turned to his right and headed for the room. The door was locked, and curtains inside prevented him from seeing anything through the slim entry window. He turned back to the nurse who had picked up the phone. "What the HELL is going on? I demand to be allowed in there right NOW!"

Dr. Dunmeier came into the ICU station at that moment and held up his hands to Sam, "Please! There's other patients here. Stay calm."

"Open. This. Door!" Sam insisted, phone in hand. "Or I'm calling the cops right now."

Dr. Dunmeier held a key fob to the door, and it clicked. He looked at Sam and said, "Please put on a gown and mask inside. We need to try to limit the challenge to David's immune system at this time."

Sam put his phone away and moved inside with the doctor. Dr. Dunmeier pointed out the packaged light yellow Tyvek coverall gowns and started to put on his own.

"I'm sorry that I couldn't give you a direct answer sooner. David's fine, but the treatment had some unusual, extraordinary, side-effects on him."

"And you couldn't tell me anything?" Sam said, "That's

criminal. Let me see him!" As soon as he tied on his mask and gown, he reached to open the curtain.

"Wait! Sam!"

But it was too late. The curtain swished back on its track and there was David, or what used to be David. A humanoid form lay on its back on sterile, white sheets under a blue gown. The smell of alcohol and iodine was pricked by something else unusual—organic, unsavory, but not fetid. His eyes were closed in sleep by wrinkled, pale lids, and he had IV lines and monitor probes on both arm-like limbs, and a slim, transparent tube delivering oxygen to his nostrils—or what could have passed for nostrils. Monitors quietly displayed their readings and IV pumps whirred. The body looked shorter than David had been, and its legs and arms appeared bonier. Hair had fallen out entirely, and the exposed skin was yellowish-pink and wrinkled. His eyes were enormous against their sunken sockets ... or was it that his nose and jaw were longer? There were angry red lines in his skin around his nose, mouth, over his eyes, and up the center of his scalp. The space between his nose and mouth bulged outward, and his nasal openings stretched apart from each other. Sam's eyes drifted down in horror to David's left hand, and he saw that the fingers were bony and pale. The pinky was shriveled with thick sheets of skin sloughing off. The feet were yellowish with thick sheets of flaky skin lifting and hanging and the toes were hideously long with blackened, thick, sharp nails. The creature, which could only be David, slept peacefully, but he looked more like a Holocaust victim than a thriving cancer patient.

Sam's hand tightened on the edge of the curtain and his mouth dropped open. "Whhaaaattt in the hoooolllyyy fuck?!" He slowly hugged his arms to himself as his eyes surveyed and resurveyed his dear friend, searching for something familiar. Tears misted his vision and he turned to the doctor, fire in his stare, "What the hell have you done to him?"

Dr. Dunmeier had taken off his glasses and slumped down in a chair against the wall. "Sam, I wasn't lying about David's improvement. Please calm down and let me explain."

Sam stood over Dunmeier, looking down in rage, teetering on the precipice of violence.

Finally, the doctor met his fuming gaze and motioned to the stool by David's left hand. "Please. Sit. Let's talk this out quietly and if you still want to beat me up, I'll still be here."

Sam sat down slowly while staring at David's hand. He wanted to hold it, but the sickly-looking limb repulsed him. His own fingers felt sticky with the need to wash at just the sight of the puffy, dangling flesh. He folded his arms across his chest and tucked his hands up under his armpits. Then he glared back at the doctor.

Dr. Dunmeier closed his eyes and pinched the top of his nose as though nursing a headache. "David's sedated. We've kept him sedated for the past few days. It was necessary to help slow and control the treatment, as hard as that might be to believe. His cancer is, as far as our scans show, almost gone. His liver is being replaced by a new liver. Likewise his pancreas, lungs, lymphatic system . . . everything is renewing. The treatment is working far faster than we anticipated. However . . . there was a miscommunication. The DNA template for his treatment was, well, confused with another patient's template."

"Whose?"

"Well, actually, not who, but what . . ." Dr. Dunmeier looked down, "It was confused with an animal that had the same protocol designation."

Sam sneered at the doctor as though hearing a lame excuse from a conniving teen. "What?"

"David's alterations are being patterned after a golden eagle," Dr. Dunmeier replied.

Sam looked back at David and surveyed him once again. He'd taken graduate level zoology and biology courses. The elongating face, ridges over his bulbous eyes, the boniness of his limbs—they did make David resemble a plucked bird. But, really?

He turned back to the doctor, "Come on? What kind of sick joke is this? You can't turn a person into a bird! You're just making shit up, thinking I'll be duped into false hope. What kind of sick bast—?"

"Quiet!" Dunmeier worked his jaw in consternation. "Look! I've concealed this from my staff, from you, and from the world for the past few days. I've tried to come up with a way to stop or reverse this and save face, but I can't. Human tissue cultures are studied in parallel with research animal tissue cultures. It helps us to tweak the process, learn the nuances, and improve the treatments. It's rare, but sometimes there is even cross-compatibility. There was a mix-up, and he received the right treatment only intended for a research animal."

Sam spat out, "You can't stop it?"

Dunmeier held up his hand firmly, his bloodshot eyes wide and staring Sam down. "The treatment controls we created were made for David's template, not this one. I'm coming clean so that we can have more options on the table. Now you need to calm the hell down and help me help David!"

Sam stared at him with wide eyes, letting the doctor's words sink in. He slowly looked over David's shriveled, grotesque form again.

Dr. Dunmeier continued, "Look at his hands . . . one doesn't have to be an ornithologist to see the similarities to a chicken's wing tip. And look down at your feet. See that bag?"

Sam looked at it confused. It was clear vinyl bag full of white liquid. "Yeah?"

"That's David's urine. What does it resemble?"

Everyone knows that bird droppings have white liquid in them, and Sam had certainly seen copious quantities of bird poop during the course of his duties as a biologist. "Bird shit?"

Dr. Dunmeier leaned forward. "Don't believe me? Let me show you . . ."

The doctor wheeled closer on his stool and lifted David's gown. Sam's eyes followed the tubing from the bag up to the bed, over David's left leg, and into his groin. He saw a blur of tape and skin and quickly looked away. He wasn't ready for that level of detail yet.

Sam's face went pale but his eyes were red with angst. He struggled to accept what he was seeing and being told. He said with a look of doubt, "What can I possibly do?"

Dr. Dunmeier continued, "Be here for him now. I still have to explain all of this to him. I need you to help me do that. He has a very important decision to make."

Sam looked over David's face again. It was difficult to recognize, but there were still touches of David there. He pulled his right hand out of his armpit and reached out, tentatively taking David's left hand in his. The flesh was very warm and soft, despite how sickly it appeared. David sighed deeply and squeezed back slowly, letting out a mumbled groan that was off-pitch from his normal voice.

Sam had his eyes fixed on his friend. "I'm going to stay here until he wakes up. You have a problem with that doctor?"

"Nope. Just do me a favor. Call me as soon as he wakes up." Dr. Dunmeier scribbled his cellphone number on the back of a business card, and handed it to Sam.

The day went by slowly. Normally, Sam would pass the time playing with his phone, but David's uncanny appearance riveted his attention like a motorist gawking at a car accident. He stung with guilt for being initially repulsed, but this faded as he grew accustomed to the knowledge that his friend really was somewhere under the sagging flesh.

Sam reviewed the times they'd had together: screwing

around in class back in high school, the camping trips, the fun times drinking in college, and the recent period of facing David's cancer together. He had always been best friends with David, like a brother. But now he felt even closer. They'd been spending a lot of time together, and while being alone was sometimes nice, he could see, now, why some people couldn't be alone. The constant companionship had filled his life and given him something, someone, to care intimately about outside of himself. And that person cared back. It was a wholeness that he hadn't felt before. He didn't want David to die—partly for David's sake but also for his own.

Sam peeked under David's loose hospital gown, wondering how he looked. He was surprised to see that although David's extremities looked bony, his chest was thick and taut. He felt a twinge of embarrassment, wondering if David would appreciate him looking, but he tentatively explored further. He gently rested a hand on David's chest and realized that it was convex and firm in the center, as though he had already begun growing the keel bone of a bird's breast. It was very shallow, but it was undeniably there. He ran his hand down David's gown to his belly. David's breast was moving more at the lower end than the upper, swinging in and out with his breaths. The skin sloped off of the tip of his breast and was soft over his belly. David stirred and Sam jerked his hand back.

He looked up to see David open his mouth and let out a broken screechy moan. He slowly opened his eyes and looked back at Sam. Deep mahogany irises, flecked with gold fixated on Sam's face. The usual white sclera visible in human eyes had all but disappeared, reduced to a thin rim around the edges. As his eyelids parted, a white membrane swept outwards away from the corners of his eyes closest to his nose, then retracted back to expose his eyes again. The dark pupils narrowed, then widened. David moved his hand, and clutched Sam's firmly. The wide corners of his mouth turned upward slightly and Sam could see more clearly that all of his teeth were gone. David let out a scratchy sound that resembled human speech cadence, but was not clear enough to understand. His eyes widened and his smile disappeared as he heard his own voice.

"Auuhh ehhh unnnhhhh oooonnnggoonnngg?" He sat up and a monitor softly burred out warning tones.

Sam squeezed his hand tightly, "David, it's okay, buddy. I'm here. You've looked better but you're gonna be all right."

David studied Sam's genuine smile, his eyes flicking with short saccadic movements, taking in every nuance in his friend's face. He settled back, moving his bizarrely long lower jaw and flicking his tongue, as though trying to make sense of his altered anatomy. He lifted his right arm to his chest and probed around, then emitted a drawn out woody tone like a tenor in warm-up exercises. His stiff, bony fingers poked the skin of his throat as he did this, and he looked at Sam, watching for signs of approval as he cleared his throat and attempted to use his new avian vocal apparatus, forming deep down in his chest.

Sam smiled. "That's it, try it out buddy."

David tried again, but couldn't shape words and he winced a little, as though the effort was uncomfortable.

Just then, Dr. Dunmeier entered the room with a nurse, and they donned caps and gowns. David looked up and made excited muttering sounds. He shook his head and held up his distorted right hand in a stopping motion. Then he looked at Sam and clutched his shirt sleeve in desperation.

Dr. Dunmeier stopped short and held out his hands as he sat down. "Don't worry, David. We're not going to sedate you. We need to have a little talk."

David's huge eyes flicked with terror from the doctor to Sam to his withered limb that still clutched Sam's shirt.

Sam moved closer to David. "David, look at me. This is a shit show, but you're going to be okay. Doc says that you're winning this fight but new stuff happened. But let him tell you all about it, okay?"

David slowed his breathing and nodded. He let go of Sam's shirt and stared at his bizarre appendage, watching the fingers slowly flex and extend repeatedly as Sam sat back down by his side.

Dr. Dunmeier laid it all down for David and Sam. The treatment was curing the cancer. He had been consulting with his team members for the past 48 hours, and their best conclusions were that they could try giving the treatment that was originally developed for David, but it was very risky. In trials, when multiple treatments were given simultaneously using different templates, the results were almost always rapid, uncontrolled mutation followed by death. They predicted that once an animal had been fully transformed for some period of time that perhaps a reversal could be accomplished, but so far it had only been accomplished with cell cultures. Further, there was concern that the cancer may still be present microscopically. If they did, somehow, stop the transformation or reverse it now, the cancer could return. It could even mutate and come back more aggressively, rendering any complete cure impossible.

David fumbled for his bed's control pad but was unable to hold it and press buttons with his bony digits. Sam gently grasped the control and helped him press the button to raise his head so he could look the doctor in the eyes. He began to mutter unintelligibly, but Sam stopped him and offered a miniature dry erase board and a marker that were resting on his bed table. David wrote out sloppily, mumbling the words deep in his throat, *What should I do?*

Dr. Dunmeier looked him in the eyes and said, "David, I'm sorry this happened. It was a long shot to start with. But, frankly, this accident may have saved your life, such as it is." He moved closer and leaned his backside against the windowsill, facing David. "Remember, I gave you slim odds.

Frankly, we've not managed to save a patient that was affected by liver cancer to your degree—at least not for more than a few weeks. But this eagle template . . ." He shook his head. "It's working far better than anything we've ever seen, and you can bet that we want to figure out why. Be that is it may, you may not want to live as a bird." The doctor's eyes wandered over David's twisted form. "Honestly, we've never seen such a radical transformation in a human before, and we don't know if you'll survive or, if you do, whether you'll still be you, mentally, not to mention physically." He smiled slightly and began speaking faster, "You're the first human to go through this. It's our first chance to be able to communicate with a subject—" He paused as his eyes met David's. "Well, with someone, that's going through this process."

Dunmeier cleared his throat and continued with a more reserved tone, "The largest transformations we've seen are from one animal species to another in the same taxonomic family. Birds and humans aren't even in the same taxonomic class! Deep down, though, all animals work from the same basic components that make up DNA, so it's not impossible that this could work. It really comes down to the order and speed of systemic changes. But we can expect problems, and we'll just have to take care of them when they surface."

Dr. Dunmeier stopped, and looked down at his feet to allow time for his words to sink in. David had been studying his deformed hands again, but then he stopped and looked back up at the doctor. His pen squeaked on the dry erase board: *So I'm gonna be a bird.*

Dr. Dunmeier frowned and looked at the floor. "Unfortunately, yes. I think it's the safest option. Again, we can switch to your original treatment, your human template, which would likely reverse what's happening, but would likely kill you—and not in a pretty way. Or, continue this treatment to its conclusion." The doctor stepped closer, his lean form blocking the light over David's face. "In my opinion, that's the safest option for your life. The other choice just preserves your humanity a little longer. Perhaps someday, down the road, we could try a reversal therapy, but we have many more animal trials to do before I'd feel safe suggesting that."

David wiggled his long pale fingers. His pinky and ring fingers had nearly shriveled away while his index and middle finger were fusing together and becoming pointed. His thumb had shrunken and become tapered. He could barely bend any of his digits because they were stiffening, yet none of this was painful. He pulled his knees up toward his chest and delicately ran his pointy hands down his shins to his bony, scaly toes and claws. He drew a deep breath and cool air filled his chest. His heart thumped faster, and blood pulsed through his thick pecs and shoulders. Such a surge of blood pressure would have been dangerous to any other person but to him it was invigorating. He felt warm and alive, like he could get up and run a race. It was almost as if he could feel his cells dividing, millions at a time, constructing his new body. He looked so sickly and freakish but was stronger than he had been in weeks, maybe even years. He didn't want to lose his soaring vitality, but his mind reeled at the possibilities of life as a bird. He really didn't know much about birds, but who hadn't ever dreamed, even fleetingly, of being one?

He nodded his head and scribbled, *Plan B. Ride this out.*

Sam squeezed David's hand. "Hey, bud, I'm gonna contact a raptor guy I know at the Department, if that's okay. He's a falconer. He's had birds since he was a kid. He'll be able to help us understand all of this. Don't worry—I'm gonna be here every step of the way with ya."

David reached out for a hug from Sam. He wrapped his left arm around and pulled Sam's chest close to his face. He made a stifled churring sound in his throat and with great effort, squeaked out, "Thaaannkthh . . . Hhhhhaaaam . . ." Tears formed in his eyes. "Lllluuv . . . Yyooo . . ."

Dr. Dunmeier stirred, stood up straight, and quietly left

the room, closing the door behind him.

Sam was warmed by the simple, barely intelligible words, spoken with such great effort. He knew that he loved David too and in that moment his soul stood as still as a windless lake. As he hugged David close he remembered a time, back in the '90s, when they sat beside Holden Lake in the Cascades, watching the stars come out. They had a portable CD player with them and were singing to some of their favorite songs and skipping stones. It was a mix that David had made and the last song was "Wherever You Will Go" by The Calling. Sam listened and watched as David skipped one more stone that skipped far into the black night. The chaotic ripples faded leaving a still, dark starry sky reflected in the lake. At that moment the last guitar notes faded out and all stood still, save the chirping of crickets. The Milky Way spilled out above them and at their feet in the watery mirror. Neither one of them moved or spoke for minutes—they just sat shoulder to shoulder and heard each other breathing. Sam knew at the time, years ago, that he loved David. The words of the song stayed with him—he would always be close to his friend through whatever, even if they never moved beyond friendship.

Sam's eyes moistened and he hugged harder. "Love you too David. Have for a long time. You're more than a friend... more than a brother to me. We'll go through this together." He wanted to say more, but he couldn't quite put the words to the ache in his heart. He knew that without David, life would be empty. It didn't matter what he looked like or how difficult the future would be together. The vast physical differences might make it difficult to classify their relationship in terms for others to understand. He quietly contemplated what it would mean to the shape of his life, his home, and his career to care for David, possibly for the rest of his life. It seemed a small price to pay to have David by his side and build their own special existence. Indeed, he couldn't see doing anything else.

Chapter 8
Challenges and Changes

W ITHOUT SEDATION, DAVID STARTED TO cope with his rapidly changing body. He became increasingly restless, and after a few days he refused to stay in bed at all. As he described on his white board: *Have to move around. Like a baby learning to walk and fly.*

It made sense to the doctors, since it was well known that normal neural development relied upon near constant motor activity in young animals. Plus, the longer he stayed in bed, the greater the risk of complications such as bed sores, pneumonia, and muscle atrophy. But they weren't certain how to accommodate his increased freedom. How would he sit? How would he stand? What if he fell and hurt himself? How would he use the bathroom? The questions were non-stop, and the legal advisors and administration were at their wits end to keep up. When the research director learned that Sam had contacted Steve, his falconer friend, a moratorium was placed on any press releases or further contact with anyone outside of the hospital about David's treatment. Nobody could take photos, take video, make social network posts, or talk to anyone out side the facility about David.

But David wouldn't wait for meetings and focus groups to give him permission to push himself. He rose out of bed one day and simply refused to get back in. He staggered around on his shaky legs, knowing that the hospital would have to listen and bend to his will if he forced the issue.

He was right. They couldn't keep him in bed, so by day seven post-treatment, they moved him to a larger room with padded walls and floor to satisfy legal liability concerns for harming himself. The psychologists felt that the strain of such a transformation would be too much for most people to bare. He insisted that he felt wonderful and had no suicidal thoughts, but that didn't keep them from monitoring him by video surveillance twenty-four hours a day. In addition to a psychologist, experts in physical therapy, neurology, pulmonology, cardiology, and many other disciplines of medicine were assembled into a think-tank to respond to problems as they occurred. Soon they found it necessary to also add experts in avian medicine and comparative anatomy. The committee held daily rounds to answer each other's questions and plan out David's treatment.

Because David's transformation was going smoothly, Sam and David had to chuckle about all the curious scientists and doctors wanting to poke their fingers into his case, literally and figuratively. While the treatment team did their best to answer all of the medical questions, they had neglected to integrate experts on how eagles live and act. Naturally, David had a lot of questions about what he needed to know that his instincts wouldn't answer, so the two did their best to find answers on their own. Although it was physically difficult for David to use a computer, with Sam's help, he was able to look up information on golden eagles.

There were more mundane bodily function issues that created problems for David. While in his bed, David had a urinary catheter to collect his liquid waste. He hadn't actually had to have a bowel movement since the beginning of his treatment. This was because his body shrank while its structure was simultaneously changing. New cells formed while old ones were destroyed and broken down for energy.

Proteins are normally used for energy in birds of prey, so the process was completely normal for his new physiology. So, David's old tissues were both a source of energy and essential building blocks for creating his new form. All he had to do was take in water and key vitamins and essential amino acids that he could not manufacture himself.

The downside of metabolizing protein and losing body mass was the elimination of large amounts of nitrogen. In birds, this takes on the form of urine or urates, the white liquid portion of a bird's droppings. Meat-eating birds excrete large amounts of it and David was no exception, which created problems for the medical team.

David's catheter was difficult to maintain, particularly as his internal plumbing went through radical changes. Add to that David's insistence on being mobile and it became impossible. On top of all of that, David's bone structure changed. His hip joints spread apart and his pubic bones separated and migrated forward. His back stiffened too, the vertebrae fusing to form a stable frame for flight, and so it was difficult for him to bend at his waist. His femurs, or thigh bones, shortened and his feet stretched. It all combined to make it very difficult for him to maneuver in tight spaces, such as a bathroom, or to sit normally as one would on a toilet.

And so, when the doctors finally removed his urinary catheter on day nine, they provided David with a makeshift portable toilet in the corner of his room. It was a basically a sanitary bucket sunk into a platform so that the opening was at foot level when David squatted over it. There was a curved plastic backsplash in the corner that would funnel stray wastes into the bucket. It had been designed with input from Sam's friend, Steve, based on his knowledge of keeping golden eagles and knowing that they tend to spurt their droppings horizontally when pooping. So with this in place, David had to learn how to poop like a bird. It was a very strange, conflicted sensation for him at first, but one that pressure in his cloaca, which serves the dual purpose of bladder and rectum in birds, would not let him procrastinate about.

The first time he performed the task, he made everyone leave the room and he had Sam cover the video camera. Some things he just had to explore alone. On one hand he had the old habit of standing to urinate. But he also had innate avian instincts that, he found, were more comfortable to follow in uniquely avian moments like these. Those instincts told him to bend forward, lift his rear, and press. So he followed his instincts (and the visuals from some YouTube videos of eagles pooping) and spurt out his first bird dropping. It was clumsy, and messy, particularly since his cloaca had not fully formed and there was not a completed vent orifice to direct the wastes as gracefully as an eagle. But it got the job done and it was tremendously satisfying to relieve himself without a catheter in the way.

David had found, with some trepidation, that his genitalia was changing too. His testicles pulled up deep inside of his belly and he couldn't see or touch them anymore. The urinary catheter had migrated with his penis downward toward his anus and the skin where his scrotum hung began to moisten and sink inward around day seven. David had read about the cloaca of birds, and it freaked him out a little. On one hand, it was more efficient to have just one hole for elimination that pretty much took care of itself. On the other, it sort of resembled a vagina which, to David, was as uncharted a territory to explore as becoming a bird. But most of the discomfort was the thought of losing what had always been a very familiar part of who he was, what defined him, at least physically, as a male, and how his sex drive was satisfied.

At this point, David realized that he was falling out of touch with his sexuality, which had taken half his life to come to terms with already. It was more important than just his superficial physical appearance. For someone unfamiliar with birds, the change was akin to feminization. He had no problem with other biologically male friends identifying as female, but he had never doubted his male gender identity before. Now he was uncertain what sex or gender he was, holding on to his pronoun simply because its what he was used to. And, it almost goes without saying, he had no idea how sexual intercourse would work or if he would ever care to engage in it again.

Despite the confusion, though, deep down David still felt fading remnants of himself and his preferences. David and Sam had discussed women before, usually during late-night, beer-soaked, philosophizing. They were both gay but at slightly different points on the spectrum. Sam admired women's physical attributes. He just preferred the company of men.

David, on the other hand, was not aroused by feminine anatomy at all, and barely so by male anatomy, for that matter. He had women as friends and respected them as coworkers, but he largely ignored their physical attributes. It wasn't a conscious effort, he just never cared how people of either gender looked. In his friendships with men or women, it was character that attracted or repelled him the most. He preferred people he could talk to and trust with his feelings without fear of judgment or betrayal. His lack of arousal by physical attributes worried him as a teen but later, with exposure to accepting viewpoints in college, he became comfortable with his own homosexual orientation coupled with a sex drive that was less physically-driven than most of his male peers. For him, it felt natural and no one had a right to question that.

David brooded on all of this as he perched in the pre-dawn darkness of the ninth day. It all settled for him when he realized that his cloaca was nearly formed and there was nothing he could do about it anyway. He was not defined solely by his outward form, and he knew he could adapt. Anyway, he hadn't had the urge for sex for weeks—since before his illness had first begun. He had much more important problems to worry about, so he pushed that topic out of his mind.

David also struggled with communication. He practiced using his new voice all the time, producing screeches and guttural, wooden, raspy tones with exhausting effort. Despite this, his ability to speak intelligibly diminished. During these efforts, ultimately, his voice would crack, and he would slump in frustration wondering why he couldn't push out words.

He researched how birds make sounds and discovered that his new voice box, called a syrinx, was located deep in his chest, down between his lungs. He no longer had vocal cords or a larynx like humans. He could shape sounds but unlike songbirds or parrots, the vocal abilities of eagles and other birds of prey is very limited. To compound matters, by day seven, David also found it impossible to hold a pen. The outside two fingers of each hand shriveled while the index and middle fingers grew together and stiffened to form wingtips. His thumb had shortened and become pointed too. The lack of two-way communication frustrated him and contributed to a rising panic within him his humanity was smothered by his new bird body. Unless something was done quickly, he would be trapped inside, cut off from two-way conversation, and lose his mind.

David's changes outpaced the ability of the research team to respond. They were simply not prepared to create new furniture and technology to adapt to him. Much to Dr. Dunmeier's chagrin, David added Jim Truskie, David's retired boss, to his power of attorney and had Sam contact him to see about creating a solution to the communication problem. Jim had a background in adapting technology for the disabled, so he leapt at the chance to help, and within a few days, he was in David's hospital room with a customized large format keyboard. They laid the keyboard on the floor with a large computer monitor on the wall. David immediately started to use his naked wingtips to tap out letters.

Jim remarked, "He looks as excited as my son when he received his first computer at six years old. He pecked out letters just as furiously!"

But Sam saw a problem, and he stopped David. "Hey, buddy, you're probably not going to be able to use your wings to type. You know, once they grow feathers? Jim says that you should be able to use your feet on these buttons too. Give it a try."

David cocked his head slightly and started punching out letters awkwardly using his clenched toes. As he started to punch out words on the keyboard, word suggestions appeared at the bottom of the screen and he selected them with special function keys along the bottom of the keyboard.

He let out an excited chirp and slowly typed out, *Thanks, Jim. You don't know how much this helps!*

There was also a tall thin joystick at the top of the keyboard that David could use to point and click. He figured out quite naturally that it was intended for his beak, and in moments he was browsing the Internet.

Jim stood back and admired David's skill at using his new computer. He also marveled at David's new appearance.

Barely a week had passed, and yet no one would know that this odd creature had been a human, much less recognize it as David. He stood at half his former size. His skin varied from yellowish-pink to yellowish-blue with fine wrinkles around his joints. Dimples appeared in evenly spaced networks across his body, each containing a gray, cottony feather. As he shrank, the dimples moved closer together and he gradually formed a dense covering of fluff, just like a downy eagle chick.

As his body changed, David's posture slumped further over and his feet and toes continued to stretch and thin into closer facsimiles of the lower legs and feet of a bird of prey.

His neck was twice as long, proportional to his body, as it had been before and had a grotesque s-curve to it. He could turn his head around and look over his back. His trachea and neck muscles were visible through his thin, soft bird skin. His eyes were enormous in proportion to his head and developed dark, broad rings that were visible under his skin. These were termed "scleral ossicles" and formed a support structure for his huge bird eyes that could no longer fit within his skull. His nose stretched out and the skin transitioned forward to a scaly yellow and then a smooth, hard dark gray. Red tracts of skin were still present around the base of his forming beak, around his ears, and down the back of his head and neck. These lines were sites of rapid cell division, spreading avian flesh out over his shrinking and withering human form. His earlobes withered and fell off leaving simple round holes at the back corners of his skull. His modesty compelled him to wear a gown and a diaper when he had visitors.

Overall, David looked like a giant plucked turkey wearing vestiges of human clothing.

Sam saw Jim's barely perceptible shudder and said, "I know, it's tough to see him like this isn't it? I had the same reaction when I first saw him, and he wasn't nearly so progressed. Here's what he's going to look like." Sam held up his cellphone with a photo of a golden eagle.

Jim admired the image and smiled. "Wow!"

Sam chuckled, "I know. Hard to believe that something so beautiful looks so ugly underneath those feathers." David spun his head around 180 degrees and glared at them. "Hey, bud, you know you're beautiful and I love ya. Hell, you're not getting any sympathy from me. You're going to look way more handsome than me pretty soon."

While Jim chuckled at this, David typed out: *You bet I will! And I'll be able to peck your eyes out if you make fun of me.*

As David resumed his computer research, Jim asked, "He still acts like the same old David. Is he losing his faculties?

His memories? Is he, I dunno, turning into a bird brain?"

Sam said quietly, "So far, so good. They test him a little bit every day, and he still seems as sharp as ever. They've found that his memory seems intact, too—we talk about growing up, and stuff we did as kids. He hasn't been able to say much but he acts like he knows what I'm talking about."

Jim nodded and rocked on his heels. "Incredible."

Sam went on. "He does have some amazing new abilities. They say that his spatial awareness is off the charts." He held up a transparent plastic board with letters and numbers on it. "They show him pictures of optical illusions and ask questions and he taps on this alphabet board to give his answers. They also toss bean bags at him and have him catch them in his beak or feet. His coordination is still catching up but his eyes seem to be giving him details that we can only imagine."

"I bet the eye doc here must be blown away," Jim said.

Sam chuckled. "Yeah, they brought this specialist in from another clinic. He looked pretty freaked out at first, like David was going to eat him. But pretty quick, he pulled out all his tools and oohed and ahhed. He looked like I do when I shop for a new fishing pole."

Jim laughed.

"Yeah, really blew him away. And this neurologist did what they called nerve conduction and perceptual tests. His sight is lightning fast—about 3-4 times faster than us. He aced their 3d puzzles really quick too. It's like he doesn't have to think about it—he just looks and reacts and gets it right every time. Hard to imagine what it's like in his head. It's gonna be fun to be able to chat with him easier now."

"Amazing!" Jim stood with mouth open in wonder. "Hard to imagine. And look at him taking it so gracefully." He walked over to David and placed a hand on his left shoulder.

David cocked his partially-beaked face upwards and chirped awkwardly. He typed on the keyboard: *Thank you,*

Jim. I really appreciate this. I'm a freak right now . . . hopefully easier to look at soon. Now I know how it feels to be a piece of software that's debugged in production.

Jim chuckled, "Nice to see you still have a sense of humor. Speaking of debugging, this keyboard is just a prototype. I'm going to work out something more portable for you soon. Just need some time to work it out."

David nodded and placed his wingtip on Jim's hand.

Jim looked down at David and said warmly, "Hey, listen, last time I saw you, I sensed you were in a rut. I gave you some advice to take your life back. I had no idea what you were going through . . . how life was literally slipping through your fingers."

David typed: *Neither did I, Jim. But I'm taking your advice. Not gonna let this stop me from living.*

Jim rubbed David's shoulder while his eyes moistened and his cheeks flushed with emotion. "Yeah, I see it. You're an inspiration to us all. You stay in touch with me now. Take care of yourself and I'll be back. Good luck, buddy."

Chapter 9
Paleopulmania

IN THE EARLY DARK HOURS of day fourteen, David slept soundly. He tended to sleep as much as sixteen hours a day, which was not unusual for nestling birds of prey. He found it most comfortable to simply lay down on his breast in a corner, with his head turned 180 degrees and resting on his back. He often dreamed of flying over stunning landscapes, but this morning his dreams involved working at the office, battling against a hard deadline.

David hurried to and fro in a half-bird, half-human state, fumbling to get things done in a human work environment. The building was different—it had a large central space that spanned from the ground floor to the top. Instead of walking to various places in the building, he would step off into this space and fly between floors as if nothing could be more natural. At one point, he had to print a report and couldn't find a functioning printer. He flew floor to floor, jogged around, and tried desperately to find a computer that would connect or a printer that had paper. The frenetic pace and increasing stress made him breathe hard and sleep fitfully.

Outside of his dream, down the hallway from his room, a nurse's station displayed his vital signs and muscle activity on monitors. While nothing could be considered routine with David, the staff had grown accustomed to frequent jumps in his heart rate as his dreams took him to extremes of imagined activity. He would twitch, vocalize, sometimes even fall over and wake up. The nurses tried to limit entering his room and checking on him, since this would further disrupt his sleep.

The neurologists and psychologists on his treatment team presumed that his intense dreams were the result of his brain sorting out millions of new connections while his memory remained intact. New instincts combined with his existing habits and knowledge to form new amalgams—hybridized emotional response paths and physical behaviors more fitting to his avian anatomy.

But tests revealed that David's existing memories also changed. He could remember events, but he had difficulty remembering sensory elements such as tastes, smells, and the details of how he performed physical tasks. It made sense to the team that he would lose these, since he had also lost the corresponding human anatomy for these parts of his existence. Initially, David was largely oblivious to the finer perceptual changes until questioned and tested. It finally hit home when he realized that he couldn't remember what strawberries tasted like. Strawberry shortcake had been one of his favorite desserts, but now the sweet and fresh flavor combination didn't make sense, and he couldn't clearly recall how it tasted. It was another sobering episode of learning how much of his humanity was slipping away.

Beyond the changes to his appearance and communication abilities, his worldly perceptions and preferences changed—the things that, in part, defined him as David. He decided to hold on to as much of himself as he could for as long as he could, though he was aware he couldn't stop the process. He also concentrated on the positives, such as all the other new senses and abilities he had yet to explore. He hadn't had an appetite, anyway, so he couldn't be sure that his memory of smells and tastes wouldn't return when he once again became hungry.

But at the moment, it wasn't his mind that was the problem. A monitor beeped and the duty nurse looked up at the infrared-enhanced video feed. David pumped his wing-like limbs and gaped his mouth rhythmically. At first, it was like another of his intense flight dreams. His heart rate had risen to 250 beats per minute, normal for an active eagle, as she had been informed. But his breathing rate was off—far higher than the usual thirty breaths per minute. She felt a cold panic on her brow as his breathing became faster and shallower. Then his eyes opened and his head flipped forward as and he squawked and gasped. His heart rate sank: *120 . . . 90 . . . 80 . . . 60.*

"Shit!" she blurted out as her eyes widened. She ran toward David's room, shouting back to another nurse, "Code blue on birdman! Call the team!"

By the time they burst into David's room, he lay sprawled on his back and wasn't breathing at all. His pupils were wide, and his beak was open. The arriving ER doctor shouted, "Airway! Airway!" and an assistant handed him a large tube while another opened David's beak. By this time, David had what looked mostly like a beak and a firm, pointy avian tongue. It helped David now because it made for simpler exposure of his glottis, the entrance to his trachea. The doctor quickly slid a breathing tube into his trachea, hooked it to a breathing bag, and started pumping.

A male ER nurse listened to David's breast with a stethoscope and wedged fingers under his right wingpit to feel his pulse. "I'm getting a heartbeat of forty-five, faint. Thready brachial pulse."

The ER doc checked David's huge dilated pupils and saw no response. "Bag him every four, get a stretcher in here!"

Within moments the ER team had transferred David's seventy-five pound body to a stretcher and then to a gurney, and he was wheeling down the hallway to an ER bay. After he was hooked up to oxygen and a mechanical ventilator, his skin changed from bluish to a pale shade of pinkish yellow again, and his heart rate climbed to eighty. In a few more minutes, he took his first spasmodic breaths on his own and gagged on his tube. His pupils became responsive, and he blinked and looked around in horror. He let out a wild screech, his syrinx allowing him to make sounds despite the tube in his trachea, and flailed his featherless wings in primitive terror. The heart monitor bleated out warnings as he overwhelmed the usual human rate thresholds. Two men held him securely until he stopped shuddering, and his vital signs slowed again.

The ER doc leaned in and said, "David, you're gonna be okay. You stopped breathing, so we had to hook you up to a ventilator. But you're breathing on your own now again, and you're going to be fine. We're not sure why you stopped breathing. We're activating the team, and we'll figure this out. In the meantime, just lay back, stay calm. Nod if you understand."

It took David an inordinately long time to process the doctor's words. Last he remembered, he was in his work dream and it had taken a bizarre turn when the rooms filled with water until he was struggling to stay above it. At the end, he was submerged and drowning. The shock of waking up someplace completely different added to his disorientation. The noise and bustle of the doctors, nurses, and life support equipment was too much for his acute senses to bear.

His nictitating membranes, the avian third eyelid, flicked rapidly over his wide fearful eyes. Laying on his back was unnatural for a bird and it was difficult to breathe, as though his chest was heavy and he didn't have space for air. Despite that, his human sensibilities told him that these were medical personnel trying to save his life, and he managed to scarcely suppress the heart-surging, mind-toppling sense of vulnerability generated by his avian instincts. Waves of panic pervaded him as though he would fall off a precipice into certain doom—like his life was in immediate jeopardy. He was on the verge of flailing again and the doctor recognized this in David's darting eyes and trembling wings.

Gradually, David's human thoughts surfaced from the chaotic depths of white blinding horror perceived by his avian senses. Rational thought returned in fits and spasms, and it took all of his mental effort to keep from sinking back into panic. He couldn't communicate without his keyboard, so he just had to get a grip, cooperate, and listen.

The doctor put his face closer and said firmly, "David, Do you understand me?"

David's grip on humanity grew stronger when he heard the doctor's commanding voice. He closed his eyes and concentrated, struggling to overcome the firing avian neurons that were telling him to flee the dangers. He slowly nodded his beak and spasmed against the breathing machine to take a deep breath on his own.

"Stop the ventilator, let him breathe on his own," the ER doctor said to a nurse.

One of the interns interrupted, "Doctor Phillips, remember our briefing on avian respiratory anatomy? Maybe those new systems are taking over. Look at his breathing effort and how his abdomen is reacting. They mentioned that birds have more difficulty breathing in dorsal recumbency, too."

Doctor Phillips noticed that David was taking deep, powerful inhalations and exhaling quickly. He had suspected acidosis or airway constriction, but the drugs they had given didn't help. Also, the skin of his sparsely covered, wrinkled belly would expand outward with each exhalation, as though it were filled with air. No human should breathe this way. He looked into David's eyes.

"David, is it hard for you to inhale?" David nodded.

Dr. Phillips asked, "Would you like to try laying on your belly?"

David nodded again. The nurses and doctors helped him

roll over while they moved his sensor leads. As soon as David was on his breast he breathed smoothly, and his panic subsided. Dr. Phillips raised his eyebrows with surprise at how quickly David improved. "Excellent work, Barton. I'm glad someone did their homework. We'll get some images in a bit and confirm it, but it looks like his air sacs have taken over respiratory function."

In minutes, Dr. Dunmeier arrived and checked over David's status. He removed the breathing tube, and they wheeled David to the radiology department for CT imaging. By the time they were done, and David returned to his room, Sam arrived and joined in on a discussion with Dr. Dunmeier. David squatted on his bird legs on the padded floor of his room, breathing normally while Sam sat cross-legged by his side hugging him close.

Dr. Dunmeier explained: "We've confirmed that David's diaphragm, a muscular wall between his abdomen and chest, thinned and ruptured. The sudden change in pressure caused the human vestiges of his lungs to expand and rupture also. In people, this is called emphysema and it makes it very difficult to breathe and can kill you. With birds, the condition is normal but for some reason there was a long delay before David's avian physiology asserted itself. Birds have a different system for sensing concentrations of oxygen and carbon dioxide in the bloodstream. One of these involves sensors in their parabronchi—a network of air passages that pass through their lungs. These sensory tissues may not have been triggered because David used his human lungs until the rupture occurred. Once we started breathing for David it expanded his unused airsacs, opened those airways, and his avian systems took over."

David nodded and typed out: *I dreamed I was drowning.*

Dr. Dunmeier replied, "Yes, it was probably a bit like having the wind knocked out of you. Those airsacs just weren't filling on their own, and we almost lost you."

David replied on his keyboard: *Thank you, doctor. It feels weird. Like air is all over inside of me.*

Dr. Dunmeier cocked his head a little. "It is! People breathe by expanding and contracting their lungs, which are like balloons full of thousands of tiny sacs. But bird lungs are more like filters. When I breathe in the air goes into my lungs, sits there a moment, then flows out—always in two directions. When you breathe, fresh air flows through tiny passages in your lungs, always in one direction whether you breathe in or out. Your airsacs move the air around to do this. The blood vessels lining those tiny air passages in your lungs also flows at perpendicular angles to the flow of the air." The doctor raised his eyebrows with scientific fascination and said, "It makes you far more efficient at gas exchange which, by the way, is exactly what you need if you're going to fly."

Sam smiled at the thought of his friend flying like a bird. "Damn, dude, why should we feel sorry for you? You're going to live every kid's dream in a little while. You're gonna fly!"

David's eyes squinted a little in the suggestion of a smile. He didn't have facial muscles or beak flexibility to smile like a person any more but a person accustomed to avian body language would get the subtle message. He typed out: *Are my avian organs working now or can something like this happen again?*

Dr. Dunmeier replied, "I don't think that there should be anything more dramatic than what just happened. Your heart is essentially avian, except that you've retained your left-arching aorta instead of a right-arching one like birds have. Your respiratory system seems to be functioning well now, but we'll test you in the days ahead. Your brain, kidneys, and liver are primarily avian now. About the only critical system that hasn't transitioned is your GI tract." He stroked his curly hair and chuckled lightly as he left the room, "David, you are giving me more gray hair by the day. Pardon the pun but we'll be watching you like a hawk for any more surprises."

68   Hal Aetus

Chapter 10
Feathers

ON THE MORNING OF DAY seventeen, just a few days after his respiratory crisis, David woke up itchy. He yawned his beak and craned his neck to look around at his body and his golden brown irises rippled as he focused close at his skin. Small nubs had emerged all over his body, appearing like bluish-gray grains of rice just under his skin, each one connected to one of his downy feathers at the surface. He rubbed his beak against them and they itched when he touched them.

Feather! he thought to himself. *At last, I can stop being cold and wearing these stupid gowns.*

Since a few days after his first treatment, David was sparsely plumed in grayish fluff that emerged from a network of dimples in his skin. Everyone assumed that it was where feathers would arise later, just as eagle chicks have natal down that paves the way for their covering, or "contour," feathers. His room was kept at a constant eighty degrees Fahrenheit. Anything below that, and the dimples in David's skin would perk up like goosebumps, and his muscles would fasciculate, a tiny twitching activity that generates heat for birds. The docs had explained that he probably hadn't grown feathers because his body was still shrinking down to its final size. Feather growth required an enormous amount of energy and nutrients, plus if feathers grew too soon, they would be the wrong size for his final body dimensions.

Later that morning, Dr. Dunmeier came in and watched while a nurse checked David's weight and measurements.

"I heard that we have feathers popping out now?" he asked.

The nurse stayed focused on gently stretching David out on his back on a platform. "Yes, doctor. Take a look!"

Dunmeier stepped closer and gently rubbed the emerging bumps. David wiggled and chirped. He pulled his hand away and stepped back. "My apologies, I'll let you finish."

A laser scale projected a beam across the platform for measuring David's body length. The nurse read the measurement from the tip of his beak to the tip of his stubby, fat tail nub: "Twenty-nine point four inches. He weighs thirty-five point three pounds, doctor."

Dr. Dunmeier replied, "Well, David, your body length is not much different from yesterday and your weight loss has slowed, though still going down. It's alright—we expected that your feather growth might start when your body size stabilized."

David rolled upright and hopped down to the floor and over to his keyboard. He typed out: *What's the current prediction of my final size?*

"You should end up about two to three times larger than a normal golden eagle, but otherwise identical," Dr. Dunmeier said. "You'll lose some more weight as your bones hollow out and pneumatize."

David quickly tapped back, *Will I be able to fly?* He was happy to still be alive but being able to fly would be even better.

"There are precedents for birds of your size to fly, including, I'm told, a beast of a bird called a Haast's eagle."

David replied: *Yeah, I came across them in my research. But they're extinct!*

The doctor fidgeted in his pocket. "Yes, fair point, but

that had more to do with scarcity of food than health issues." He lifted his eyebrows and smiled wistfully. "We won't let you go extinct. But seriously, flying is going to demand a lot from your body, so you'll have to stay in peak shape to do it. Suffice it to say we're pretty sure you'll have the metabolism and anatomy to allow it. You'll have to eat a lot and we have the team working on diets for you.

"Speaking of which, now that you are starting to grow feathers, you will need extra amounts of methionine, an essential amino acid for feather growth. And you're going to have to begin eating soon. Eating raw meat is going to be a big adjustment for you. But I'm betting that your hunger coupled with your new senses will probably make that transition easier."

David flapped his stubby, fluffy wings and quickly lost his breath. *I feel an urge to use these but they feel heavy and clumsy.*

Dr. Dunmeier stroked his own chin and said, "The falconer, Steve, said that young raptors get the urge to flap as they grow out their feathers. It's probably important for you to follow that instinct and tone your muscles. In addition to your daily mobility exercises, we'll start having you work those wings."

By the next day, many of the pin-like nubs, known as blood feathers, had emerged and David could see how his baby down was attached to the tips of each one. By the third day, the feathers had emerged a couple of inches, each with a bluish waxy coating. The tip of these sheaths began to dry and crumble, and the maddening itch from this drove him to learn how to preen—the process of running the feathers through the beak, one at a time, to remove the sheaths and align their barbs.

Preening became his new obsession, and he spent most of his waking hours doing it. No sooner would he finish peeling off the sheaths of the feathers on his tail when he would feel an itching on his left wing. Once he finished there, his right wing needed attention. And so it went on, round and round his body, taking breaks to exercise or take one of his many naps throughout the day. As he nibbled and peeled away the sheaths he also unfurled and flattened out the delicate new vanes. Within a few days, his body was covered with a patchwork of down and short, soft contour feathers but his wing and tail flight feathers still had a long ways to go. But even six inch long wing feathers, when flapped energetically, produces a breeze and kick up a flurry of white flakes and stray downy feather bits that cycloned around his fluffy body.

He began to look like an eagle instead of a plucked chicken covered in gray fuzz. The soft down that originally had covered him stayed adhered to the tips of his new feathers as they grew out. The downy tips on his head feathers would dance around as he chirped and darted his beak.

David looked so silly in this stage that it was tough for Sam to keep a straight face during conversations and he often struggled not to laugh. The first time this happened, David didn't understand and shot Sam an eagle stare and cackled his annoyance. But, this only made Sam laugh harder as the delicate fluff completely ruined any intimidation.

When Sam regained control of his laughter and showed him a mirror, David sheepishly apologized and replied: *Laugh now but I'll have the last laugh when I look better than you!*

David taught himself the names of all of his feathers as he became acquainted with them. The large feathers for flight on his wings were collectively known as remiges. The outer ten, which connected to the bones of what was once his hand and fingers, were tapered and stiffer than the others. These were called primaries and would be his propellers to provide thrust for flight. The sixteen inner remiges, connected to what was once his forearm, were broader and had thinner shafts. These formed the airfoil of his wing and provide lift to keep him in the air. They were known as secondaries.

His thumb, which rested along the front edge of his wingtip, also had three feathers and was called the alula. He read that this would help keep his wing from stalling at low speeds and high angles of wing tilt during flight. His tail feathers were known as rectrices or alternately known by falconers as "deck" feathers.

Initially David had difficulty reaching his tail with his beak because his neck was still lengthening. But within a week of the emergence of his first feathers, he found that by twisting his tail forward, dropping his wing, and stretching his neck all the way back, he could almost reach them. The vertebrae in his neck were still dividing to make up the usual avian complement of fourteen as opposed to the normal human number of seven. Until that happened, he probably wouldn't have the flexibility to reach all of his feathers. By this time, his largest tail feathers were six inches long, and the feather sheaths, still intact because they were out of reach, looked like plastic straws wrapped around the lower shafts. During a visit on day twenty-one, Sam helped gently pick and rub those most unreachable blood feather sheaths. David sat with eyes closed groaning softly and occasionally wiggling his tail giving off an image of deep contentment at this special attention.

Sam remarked, "This is pretty satisfying to do . . . is it good for you too?"

David opened his eyes slightly, his wide pupils looking sleepily upwards, and he let out a soft sigh trailing into an affirmative chirp.

Sam worked down a center rectrice toward the base and felt the softer, pulpy portion. David tensed up and let out a sharp chirp.

"Oops! That part's not quite ready yet I guess," said Sam as he looked up at David's sharp eyes. David's lower lids slid up halfway and he sighed again as Sam continued to work on nearby feathers. "Hey, Isn't it about time for some wing-er-cising?"

David moved his tongue a little in and out in a swallowing motion then made a soft chirp and a head nod.

"I haven't seen this yet. Mind if I stay and watch?"

David wagged his head as if to say, *No, I don't mind.* He then arched his back and lifted his folded wings at the shoulders, giving his pectoral muscles a stretch. He twisted his tail to the right as far as it would go, dropped his wing, and reached back with his neck as far as he could. He trembled a little, softly grunting with the effort to reach his tail. There was a pop as David's neck vertebrae finally completed their division and he was finally able to extend further and grasp his outer right rectrice in his beak. He let out a content churring sound and nibbled eagerly at the feather.

Then he parted his rump feathers and exposed a small fleshy gland with a tuft of yellow-stained feathers.

"Oh, so that's your preen gland!" Sam said as he reached a finger in and tickled it a lightly. David's feathers flared and he chortled and wiggled his tail. He licked Sam's hand. "Ticklish there, eh?" Sam pulled back his hand and rubbed the light, clear oil around on his fingertips. It was smooth, odorless, and dissipated into his skin quickly.

David nibbled the oil gland and then ran his beak down his tail feathers one by one. He also twisted his head side-to-side against the gland to rub off the sheaths on his head feathers and spread the conditioning oil. Then he rubbed his cheek feathers down his wings and back to spread the oil all over. When he was through, his feathers were bouncy and shiny. He held out his wings and puffed up for Sam to admire.

Sam smiled and shook his head slowly. "You always were the prettier one, you show off."

Soon there was a knock at the door and Steve, the falconer, along with Nurse April, entered the room. David erected all of his feathers and shook hard causing bits of stray feathers and sheaths to fly around him in a dusty cloud.

Sam fell back in surprise exclaiming, "What the hell was that for?" David held his beak up high and settled all of his feathers back into place.

Steve responded, "It's called 'rousing.' All birds do that. It helps get the feathers to lay correctly. It's part of their feather care routine." David chirped and nodded.

"Well, okay, only give a guy some warning next time!" Sam said as he gave David a friendly scratch under the chin.

Steve pointed to the exercise perch in a corner of the room. "Okay! Time for exercise!"

David hopped off of his perch and plodded over toward the fatter, rope-covered exercise perch. It stood three feet high and had a narrow rope-covered ramp connecting it to the floor. David spread his wings and clambered his way up the ramp, flapping.

Sam turned his chair around to watch.

April started by massaging David's breast and shoulders for a couple of minutes. He watched her passively, as though he was only mildly paying attention. Instead, his focus was on the exercise to come. He had been doing these exercises one or two times daily, sometimes more on his own. It was always hard, but two things pushed him on.

First, there were his avian instincts. Like a restless chick in a nest, he had the urge to test his wings. The sky called to him. A place that was rounder, organic, challenging, and virtually limitless. It was where this new body belonged, not cooped up in a square room in a square building.

The second force driving him was his human desire to be whole and leave the hospital. David didn't know what his life would be, but he knew that he was tired of the hospital. And he was ready to leave his old complacence behind and push on into his new life. He looked over at Sam, who smiled back encouragingly. Whatever his life would be, he knew that it would have Sam in it. Just a friendly look from Sam sent a swell of hope and comfort through David's breast. He liked to ponder the many things that they would do together.

April completed her massage and stepped away.

"Are you ready to start, David?" asked Steve. David nodded and chirped.

Steve held up a timer and said, "Ready! Set! Go!" and the timer beeped as he pressed a button. Steve counted out "One, two, three, four! One, two, three, four . . ." to help set a pace. David flapped his stubby wings in time with the easy rhythm of about two beats per second. Within a minute David's beak dropped open, and he panted rapidly, but kept pumping his mushy muscles. After two minutes, Steve counted down, ". . . and done in ten, nine, eight, seven, six, five, four, three, two, one. Stop! Cool off for two minutes."

David stopped and drooped his wings and head, panting so hard that he honked.

Sam looked at him sympathetically. "You're making me tired just watching! Man, isn't there an easier way to do this?" Steve looked at his timer and shook his head. "Nope. Believe me, flying is harder than this. It's only tough for him now because his muscles are soft and the circulation isn't completely developed. They're starved for oxygen but exercise will take care of that."

Soon, David closed his mouth and breathed in and out through his nares again. He closed his eyes and lifted his beak. He slowly opened them after another thirty seconds and let out a sigh, indicating he was ready.

"Okay, flap faster this time, David. I want to see three beats per second okay? I know you can do it! Ready! Set! Go!"

David clutched the perch and flapped again for two minutes. This time he made it less than a minute before his beak dropped open and dripped with drool and condensation. It was a struggle, but he pushed himself and kept flapping.

"Come on, David, keep going! You can do it!" Steve shouted.

David faltered and slowed, chirping with the effort.

Sam scrambled over and crouched down in front of David, holding his arms out like wings. He started to flap along with him. "Come on, buddy, come on! Keep going! You're gonna fly soon! Think of it!"

David's eyes opened wide and he stared back at his new coach. Determination rose inside of him, and he flapped harder. He jumped up and down slightly with each flap, trying to help push his numb wings any way that he could. Sam mimicked him, bobbing up and down and flapping his arms ridiculously, but his face was serious. He had his eyes locked on David's, telling him, without any words, how much he believed in him.

A euphoric wave of energy rose up David's stretched wings, and he pressed himself further. He pumped harder and faster, letting out chirps like an athlete at his barrier.

"Stop! Stop!" came Steve's voice. They had both missed Steve's countdown, such was their concentration on each other. David stopped and drooped his throbbing wings, panting heavily. He let out a grunting chirp and sagged down on his tired legs. His heart thumped loudly in his hollow chest and Sam moved forward and support David's aching breast in his hands.

David looked up at Sam, his beak open and drooling, his tongue out and his glottis blowing hot air against Sam's face. Sam moved closer and pressed his nose to David's soft throat. "Good job, buddy, good job!" He said as he stroked David's breast feathers and patted his hot feet. David closed his eyes and laid his head down on the top of Sam's. Soon David's breathing slowed down, and he closed his beak. Sam continued to help hold him until he lifted his head and he didn't need words to read the resolve and thankfulness in David's rich brown eyes.

"You're ready to do more?" Sam asked.

David's pupils pinned smaller, and he flared his face feathers to lift his beak corners ever so slightly. It was his way of smiling. David nodded his beak and lifted his wings.

Steve held up his timer and said, "Nice work, David. Once more, slower pace. Two minutes! Ready! Set! Go!"

Chapter 11
Ins and Outs

I T WAS DAY TWENTY-TWO, JUST five days after David's feathers emerged, when he awoke in the predawn hours with a gnawing hunger. The doc was right: with feather growth came the need for food. Experiencing the forgotten sensation of hunger was, to his senses, like waking from a long, deep sleep and David was initially confused about what the pangs in his belly and the sharpness of his avian senses meant. Every stray motion and every drifting mote of dust stabbed his attention and made his muscles twitch. He was ready to spring up and grasp anything that moved and consume it faster than thought.

David's stomach churned and gurgled, forcing bubbles of gas up into his crop. The crop, David had learned, was an expandable area of his esophagus right above his breast at the base of his neck. It's where birds of prey store food for digestion. He didn't belch like a person would. Instead, his body lurched a little as it expelled gas into his crop as a silent, internal burp. Sometime later it would escape passively up his esophagus to his mouth. It was a new sensation, but it was overshadowed by his nagging urge to fill his crop with prey.

When the nurse arrived later and opened the door. David bolted off his perch and skidded to a stop on the floor. The woman lurched back in surprise before David's human thoughts caught up, and recomposed himself. He strode back to his keyboard and typed, *Need food now! Very, very hungry!*

The poor woman nervously nodded and backed through the door, slamming it shut once within the safety of the hallway. A little while later she returned with a covered tray. She set it down on the floor and lifted the cover slowly, exposing a large, plump quail with the wings and feet removed. Its body was torn open exposing dark red meat and organs. Before the cover was halfway removed, David had leaped ten feet, skidded into the tray, and seized the plump morsel in his huge powerful foot. The nurse shrieked and the lid clattered to the floor. David bit into the prey with a bloody crunch and spread his wings over his kill, all of his feathers standing on end and quivering. He slowly rotated his beak up toward the nurse, his head low and menacing, blood dripping from the hunk of meat and feathers stuffed in his maw. She shrieked and paddled her arms behind her, searching for the doorknob. In a second she slipped out of the door in a flurry of wild screams.

When David turned his face back to look at the ragged carcass in his foot, a tingling sensation squeezed the flesh under his tongue and in his cheeks. Moisture welled up in his mouth, he salivated intensely, and salty fluid pooled in the edges of his nares then dribbled down his beak. The strong Pavlovian response prepared his mouth and throat for the feast. He thought to himself that he would never have eaten a raw bird like this before, but he was so hungry, and red meat looked so appealing, that he didn't care about his old sensibilities.

David thought about chewing the chunk in his beak, but then just relaxed his jaws and quickly bolted his head forward, flipping the chunk of flesh into the back of his throat. An intense satisfaction tingled up his neck as the bolus sank down his gullet into his crop. His crop and stomach contracted and gurgled receptively, and he sighed with relief.

He quickly sank his beak into the carcass again and jerked against his talons. He heard moist crunches and wet tearing sounds as organs and ribs separated and he smelled the iron-rich blood dripping from his beak. He moved his tongue forward and tasted the fresh, cool meat. Again, he thought briefly about chewing, but remembered he didn't need to. It was a habit that was no longer necessary, and his avian systems knew what to do. He pressed his tongue further forward, pinned the meat between his tongue and upper beak, then dragged it backward. He pushed his tongue forward again, this time a pair of fleshy hooks at the back of his tongue engaged the nourishment and dragged it deep into his gullet where he swallowed it down. His crop stretched to accommodate it, and another wave of pleasure swelled through his brain—the biochemical reward for successful foraging on a very empty stomach. He loved this feeling and couldn't wait for the next bite.

David feasted without concern for table manners or cleanliness. He created a terrible mess of blood spatters and feathers, partly due to his unfamiliarity with eating like a bird, but mostly because he was too starved to care. He simply wanted to consume and keep consuming until he was packed full. He swallowed bones, skin, feathers, and everything else. As his crop filled, he slowed his pace and daintily picked off the tenderest bits of flesh instead of swallowing the feathers and larger bones.

As David finished his meal and picked sticky bits of meat from his talons, a warmth grew in his belly and radiated out through his wings, legs, and up through his head. He grew sleepy and swayed back and forth over the spattered gore. His heavy crop wobbled like a pendulum and periodically spasmed in concert with his neck. During this process, known by falconers as "putting over," he would extend his neck upwards and then scrunch downward, forcing a fresh wad of meat in his crop against the opening to his lower esophagus, sending it into his stomach bit by bit. He drifted in and out of consciousness, sleepily taking in all the strange new sensations as his stomach squeezed and gurgled around the intense chemical reactions occurring within.

Who knew it gave birds such satisfaction to be full? he thought.

If David had to compare it to anything, it would have been the feeling after sex or after the most satisfying meal he had ever had as a person. Perhaps it would get old with repetition, but he was beginning to understand what a powerful motivator this intense satisfaction would be for an animal needing to hunt and kill to survive. Regardless, he sat and basked in the endorphin-fueled afterglow of his gustatory accomplishment.

Soon, Dr. Dunmeier came in and found David in this state of bliss. David immediately smoothed his feathers down and perked up. He knew he'd have to answer for his actions. He weaved and bobbed over to the keyboard and typed out: *Sorry, Doc. Something came over me. I saw red meat and couldn't resist. Lost control but I wasn't gonna hurt her, lol.*

Dr. Dunmeier laughed nervously. "Well, I thought it might be something like that. Are you sure you can control your reactions in the future?"

David replied: *Yes. Won't happen again. Now that I know what to expect, I'll be prepared for it.*

Dr. Dunmeier nodded. "I trust you liked your food?"

David jolted as a bubble of gas rose up from his stomach into his crop. He moved his tongue in and out and tasted the intense acid. *Yep. Thanks. I never knew birds got so much pleasure from eating. Makes me sleepy, like I'm drunk.*

Dr. Dunmeier smiled, "Good! That was only about a third of what you might normally eat on a daily basis if you were a wild eagle, at your larger size of course. We're starting you out slowly to make sure everything works well first."

David typed back: *Should I worry about diseases from raw meat like that?*

Dr. Dunmeier sat down on a stool and said, "We took steps to make sure that this meat was sanitary, but our avian expert says that internal parasites are pretty uncommon in eagles. Your stomach has strong acid that kills most things. You can even digest bones. Still, I recommend that you eat carefully selected food raised from clean flocks or frozen for several days to destroy parasites. You should also not eat the upper GI tract from pigeons as it can contain a parasite that's pretty nasty for birds of prey. We'll give you a list of all of this stuff later. We also added vitamins to help with your feather growth."

David typed: *I ate the feathers too . . . I just couldn't help myself, I was so hungry. What's going to happen with those?*

Dr. Dunmeier smiled. "It's okay, you'll be fine. In about twelve to eighteen hours you should cast a pellet."

David cocked his head, and his eyes pinned slightly as he pondered the process of casting. He had read that birds of prey will form pellets of fur and feathers and regurgitate them after a meal. It sounded rather unpleasant but there was nothing he could do about it now.

David spent the morning putting over his meal from his crop to his stomach in regular intervals. He also preened and searched up more information about his digestive system. A few times he caught himself slipping into a strange state of half sleep. As he rested, one of his eyes slowly closed while he continued to read or think. Moments later a sound in the hallway jolted him to full alertness. He woke up from a state of sleep, yet he had a full memory of what he had just been thinking and reading.

David checked it out on the Internet and told Sam about it when he visited later: *It was weird. It was literally like sleeping with one eye open. I kept waking up and realizing that I'd already been awake. Sometimes it happened while I was read-*

ing, and I could recall all that I'd read, but there was still the feeling that I was waking up and seeing a wider field of view again. I looked it up and it's called unihemispheric sleep.

Sam looked puzzled. "Uni-whats-it sleep? Huh?"

David shook his head slowly and typed on: *Uni-Hemi-Spheric, meaning half your brain—like what you have!*

Sam glared in reply. "Hey, not nice, bird brain!"

David let out a beaky snicker and typed back: *I guess a lot of birds can sleep just half of their brain at a time. It makes it possible to sleep while flying long distances or while watching for predators in perpetual daylight, like summertime in the Arctic. I guess I can do it too.*

Sam laughed. "That would've come in handy in school, especially after a hard night out!"

Another aspect of eating again was that David had to come further to terms with was his bowel movements. Birds have very different plumbing than humans—all wastes, whether liquid or solid, exit through one combined organ called a cloaca. It took David's genitals and anus a while to migrate together and for several days he had problems maintaining a sanitary condition around his groin. The skin in the area had slowly deepened and his penis had shrunk and disappeared inside his cloaca. He learned to squat and spurt out white fluid, known as urates, just like he had seen in bird droppings. This happened regularly and copiously due to the metabolism of his own proteins as he shrank, an internal source of nutrition rich in nitrogen.

For a while, his pooping was less than perfect, and he could not do much to clean himself, so nurses had to clean his backside for him. He also wore a harness with diaper-like pads in it to help absorb moisture and leakage that he could not control until his cloaca completely formed. After eighteen days, the transition to a cloaca was completed including formation of a horizontal set of lips called a vent. It was located behind his legs just under his tail allowing his crotch to remain dry and clean. At first his modesty caused him to continue to wear the diapers and the gown to hide the bare wrinkled lips. However, the clothing had chafed against his growing feathers so badly that he finally ditched it, and soon his feathers did a better job of hiding his anatomy anyway.

Now with his gut full of food, he found it necessary to empty his cloaca frequently and the pressure from feces and urates was greater than before. Like any eagle, he quickly discovered that it worked well to bend over and shoot his droppings with full force horizontally instead of squatting. But whereas an eagle in the wild wouldn't care which direction, David at least had the sense to use his corner receptacle. It became a little bit of a game (there was so little to do) for him to see if he could hit the same spot repeatedly. He wondered if wild eagles ever found amusement in aiming their droppings, and becoming legendary crack-shots at shooting their excrement.

It dawned on David that eagles probably derive pleasure from eating and digesting a big meal because it might not be every day that they succeed in hunting. During lean times of the year, it would be a luxury to kill or find large prey and it meant that one might not need to hunt for a day or two. It made sense, too, that their bodies would naturally reward them with endorphins, a variety of feel-good hormones, to increase their sense of well-being and cause them to be sedentary and conserve blood flow for digestion. David's heavy contentment continued on for six hours until his stomach was mostly empty.

The next morning, David's belly was hollow and demanding again, but not as intensely as before. He began his day like others, stretching, pooping, and preening in that order. About an hour after waking, his stomach tightened. He belched and instead of tasting strong acid, as he had the day before, he tasted only dry air. He tried to resume preening but then there was a strong tightening in his jaws, forcing them open, followed by another powerful contraction of his stomach and relaxation of his crop. He felt queasy, but not as intensely as when he would throw up as a human. He lowered his head and opened his beak wide just as his stomach lurched again and his throat expanded. Then he had an urge to heave and his abdominal muscles tightened up. His breath hissed out of his closed glottis and a wad of damp feathers tumbled out of his throat onto the floor beneath his perch. Then, just as quick as the urges arrived, they were gone.

David cocked his head and studied the pellet on the floor. He licked the roof of his mouth and swallowed, surprised that it neither tasted nor smelled offensive. He fluffed his face and head feathers out, feeling a wave of relief. He roused and shook his head vigorously, then sighed and relaxed. Egesting a pellet really hadn't been so unpleasant after all. His stomach contracted and squeezed out a last bubble of gas into his crop before it quieted down. But minutes later, the dull, cold smolder of hunger returned.

So this is how it is. Food is like a drug for birds of prey. It felt incredible to stuff myself. Then I came down from that high, and now that I regurgitated my prey remains, I need another fix. This magnificent body and the gift of flight come with costs, I guess. I'm ruled by my stomach now.

As David contemplated this, he realized that he must be the first eagle to ever question if there was more to life than a full crop. He hadn't been keeping much of a diary of his experiences—just typed out short, dry notes of what was happening physically. He didn't like the exercise of writing, but he was compelled to record his thoughts on this occasion:

I don't have to be a slave to nature. Humans have overcome nature in many ways. I can still do lots of things I wanted to do as a human, things that no bird would wanted to do. And now I can do things I couldn't as a human either. I was dying before cancer struck me. I had let work become my life and forgot about dreaming about bigger things. Now I can grow those dreams again. I can live a different life. But the biggest challenge I face remains the same. It's not my health, or living up to the expectations of others, or struggling to earn a living. Even as a man in a bird's body, I still face those same issues. No, the biggest challenge I've always faced is overcoming myself. I am in control of how I live from this day forward. I can let myself be controlled by life, or I can live my life like I'm free . . .

He blinked his third eyelids to clear the thickening tear film from his eyes—an emotional response that birds would not normally express. He breathed deep, high with the euphoria of self-realization. He was strong and he pushed his hunger into the background. For the first time in weeks, he wept for happiness, bathing in the full joy of the gift of life he had received.

I will be free. Not because I can fly or because I have everything I need. I'll be free because I choose not to let anything dictate my attitude and how I am inside. Not my body, not my circumstances, not any negative people around me. I will show others this, too, and bring as much joy as I can carry on these wings.

David wasn't really sure that he could live up to all of that but for the moment, in the height of his thankfulness, he wished to see others feel as centered and as sure as himself, without having to go through the same trials.

Chapter 12
First Flight

SAM VISITED ON THE MORNING of day twenty-eight and found David shifting about restlessly on his perch. He hadn't received any food yet, and his body was not letting him forget. Conversing with Sam was a welcome distraction from his gnawing hunger and afforded him an opportunity to experience a slice of life "on the outside." Despite a window and fast Internet, he felt disconnected from the world and the normal stuff of day to day life. The routine of waking up and going to work was a distant dream from another lifetime. Although he didn't miss the grind all that much, it made him feel more normal human to hear Sam talk about his biologist duties, the quirks of his coworkers, and the frustrations of traffic. As Sam described his recent community meetings with local tribes and citizenry over salmon and eagle issues, it reminded David of food and his stomach audibly rumbled.

Sam heard it and stopped in mid-sentence. "Wow you're starving. I'm sure there's a good reason they haven't fed you yet."

David clacked out on his keyboard: *They could've told me something. The nurse checked on me a while ago, but he was new and didn't know anything.*

Sam chuckled. "You probably scared off the one who fed

you last week."

David looked at him with wide eyes. *Oh man! You might be right! Damn, I was so hungry and edgy. It's hard to ignore it when this bird body needs food.*

Sam came over and sat cross-legged on the floor by him, his fingertips gently kneading the skin under the feathers of his back. "I'm here, buddy. They say it'll get easier once you're done changing and growing feathers. Let's give 'em a few more minutes, and then I'll go and check if no one shows up."

Moments later, Steve and April knocked and entered. Steve said, "Good morning, David. Time for your exercises." Behind them, David craned his neck and riveted his eyes on a new apparatus—a low cart with a big perch on it. Steve followed his gaze and said, "Yep, that's right, you're going for a little ride. We have something special set up for you. Hop on up, and we'll go get started!"

David cocked his head. *What about food? I haven't had anything yet.*

"Yeah, I know. I had them change your feeding schedule today," Steve said. "You're going to exercise really hard, so it's best to do it on an empty stomach. Don't worry, you'll get a nice meal afterwards, and you won't have any more afternoon exercise sessions, unless you elect to do them yourself."

David looked at Sam with his wings drooped.

Sam laughed. "Aww, he looks pretty disappointed."

Steve continued, "David, your feathers are almost full grown, and you're getting too powerful to keep exercising in here. We've set up a makeshift wind tunnel in a basement hallway. It should be a safe place for you to start trying your wings. You have a lot of muscle to build, and we can't think of any better way. You should be excited; you're going to start using those wings for what they're meant for!"

David's posture perked up, and his feathers relaxed. He walked slowly over to the cart and flap-hopped up onto the perch.

"Can I come along?" Sam asked.

Steve nodded. "Of course. This won't be easy, and David will probably need the encouragement."

They rolled David through the hallways on his mobile perch, took an elevator to the basement, and wheeled down to a long hallway where a six foot fan waited at one end. About twenty feet in front of this fan was a three foot high perch. Padding covered the floor and lined the lower half of the walls.

They pushed David up to the first perch in front of the fan, and Steve tapped it with his hand. "This is your starting point, David. We'll start out with just a breeze and have you flap for two minutes. Then you'll rest for a minute and repeat at a higher intensity. We'll do this ten times or until you become too tired to continue. There's sensors in the perch. You can control wind intensity by tapping the right side of the perch for higher speed, or the left side for lower speed." Steve pointed to a wedge of padding that projected up two feet from the floor about five feet in front of the perch. "That's your shelter if something goes wrong or you just need to stop immediately. I'm also attaching this kill switch to your foot." Steve held up a red coiled plastic safety lanyard. He Velcroed it around David's right foot and inserted a key at the other end into a slot. "If you need to stop immediately, jump to the floor behind the windbreak. This key will pop out and shut everything down. Do you understand?"

David nodded his beak and gave an assuring chirp.

Steve pulled out something that looked like a leather falconry hood but with clear plastic for the cups that covered the eyes. It also had foam padding inside the portion that would cover the back of David's head.

"This was a little weird to make but the safety freaks insisted. It's hearing and eye protection for ya." He slipped it over David's beak slowly and seated it in place before pulling straps at the back to close it. "Feel okay?"

David nodded and chirped.

Steve continued, "April has a couple of things for you too."

April stepped up to David. "Okay, first I'm going to check your vital sign telemetry," April said as she pulled out a tablet. David still wore a set of three electrodes hooked to a wireless transmitter on a neck band. April handed the tablet to Steve and said, "I've set it for alarms to go off if there is a heart rate above 300, which should be more than safe for an eagle during exercise." She turned to David. "Now I need to take a small sample of blood, just a drop, and then another after your exercise session. We'll use this to measure serum lactate which will help us gauge improvements in your muscle stamina."

David was used to the myriad of blood draws, so he held out his left foot for her to access. She used a lancet that snapped and pricked the skin between two toes. She collected a drop of blood using a tiny capillary tube and applied a little pressure with a cotton ball. David looked at her with his warm brown eyes. He could see every wrinkle in her skin, every tiny blood vessel, every spasm of her irises. He knew that she was always a little scared when she had to be so close to him. He tried hard to fluff his face feathers in a hint of a smile and he winked his right eye. She blinked, and her eyes darted a little, assessing what he was trying to communicate.

Steve interpreted. "I think he's trying to put you at ease, nurse."

David chirped approvingly.

She smiled and blushed, stroking one of his warm toes. "Oh, alright. Sorry, David, I've never been around birds before this whole experience with you. I guess you can tell I'm nervous."

David thought to himself, *Yeah, and I wish I could just say it. Best I can do is this... David lifted his foot and curled his toes gently over her finger, his talons relaxed.*

Sam said, "And I recognize that. He says he understands." April clasped his foot for a moment, "You're a sweet guy, David. I haven't forgotten that you're still a person in there. I'd better run this test, but I'll be back when you finish." She rubbed his foot and set it down on the perch.

As soon as April left, Steve handed Sam a pair of goggles and some ear plugs. "Here, put these on. Safety first!" He turned to David. "Whenever you're ready, just tap the right hand-, er talon-, side sensor and you'll be in control."

David held his wings out to his sides and thumped his right foot. The giant fan whirred to life, building to a low speed. The breeze was a light and airy five miles per hour, just enough to rustle David's downy-tipped contour feathers. He spread his wings in the breeze, and his wings were buffeted by wind for the first time. His eyes widened with wonder, and he leaned forward. His feathers rippled, and then laid down flat around his head and neck.

David closed his eyes, concentrating on the wind tugging and buffeting his flight feathers. Although heavy and soft at the base, as they weren't quite full grown, they tilted and fanned, carving the wind instead of bludgeoning it like David's old body would do when he sped along on his bicycle. His body sculpted the air gracefully and it clung tightly over his streamlined shape like a second invisible skin. Hundreds of hair-like feathers, called filoplumes, were interspersed amongst his plumage. They transmitted the compression and elevation of his contour feathers to receptors in his skin, allowing him to know where air pressure was high or low at any point on his body and wings. It was a new sensation and drove home that he really was made for the sky.

David stomped down on the right button again and the fan picked up speed. He leaned further into the river of air and his wings buffeted and became lighter. The first sensation of lift was a thrill better than any steep hill on a bicycle.

Not enough, he thought, and he stomped the button again, and then again. He held his wings out stiffly and the wind lifted and fluttered his tail out behind him. Buffeted by the stiff breeze, he flapped his huge wings but his soft, blood-filled feathers were not ready for his full weight. Pain shot through the roots of his primaries causing him to wince and falter. He folded his wings and decided on a new strategy.

He pressed the left button and the breeze slowed. Steve made a flapping motion with his arms, indicating to David that he should start to exercise. David obeyed and started flapping in place just as he had in his room.

For most of his life, David had not been very athletic. He had always lacked upper body strength but he enjoyed using his legs to cycle or go on long hikes with Sam in the mountains. During the hardest hikes, he was driven forward by the anticipation of seeing new things just beyond the next corner. Now he forged ahead toward an even more intoxicating goal—flight. He was a pioneer, crossing a frontier, just like the Wright brothers or Lindbergh or Armstrong. The first human to experience completely self-powered flight without the encumbrances of artificial gadgetry. As if this weren't enough to inspire him, David also recognized that somewhere beyond the strenuous workouts, and the twists and bends of his treatment journey, there would be a new life to live and discover. With every flap, he grew closer to taking flight, both literally and figuratively.

In the hospital room, when David exercised on his perch, Sam was right there beside him, and he could hear, and see, and feel his encouragement. But now, he could barely hear him. Soon, when he would be really flying, Sam wouldn't be there with him in the air. So, David let that subtle isolation grow and envelope him. It dropped him into a deep, inner place of his thoughts where he could push himself harder and farther. He let his human mind go quiet and concentrated on the rhythm of his breast muscles pumping and the sensation of his wing strokes as his primaries cut the air to his will. He let himself be the creature of wind he was meant to be.

David's chest and belly filled with cool air which he drank eagerly through his open beak. It rushed down his trachea, whistled through his syrinx, and washed out through his lungs into his airsacs. The air sank lower and cooled his organs as he finished each inhale. As he exhaled, the air flowed forward into his neck and shoulders, and rose, hot and depleted, up his trachea and jetted out through his glottis and across his panting tongue. With each breath, in and out, vital oxygen fed his hungry chest and sharpened his mind. His heart pumped hot blood out to his demanding breast muscles and to the tips of his wings. It made him powerful. The fastest bike ride or the highest hike couldn't compare, and he hadn't even taken flight yet.

David stared ahead, growing stronger and more determined with each flap. He didn't think about how to fly, he just worked his wings like they were meant to be worked. Stretching his toes, he leaned forward and trusted his new wings, just as he had trusted his new legs as a toddler. He felt his center of gravity shift tangibly, like an invisible, heavy ball rolling forward and back between his belly and his chest. He made minute adjustments in his wing and leg posture to dampen its wobbling, and eventually to steer it. It probably helped that he wasn't a pilot and hadn't studied aeronautics. Otherwise, he might have tended to overthink the physics and forces. Instead he let his avian neurology react instinctively to his body's trajectory and attitude relative to wind and gravity. He was instinctively vying for the precise balance between controlling aerodynamic forces and letting the forces control him.

Like balancing on a bike for the first time, David's nervous system was experimenting and learning. His cerebellum, the primary center for motor coordination, was hot with flaring neurons being sculpted with each action and reaction because, although his bird body was wired for flight, it still needed experience for fine tuning.

As David felt more confident, he pressed forward and stretched his wings wider, letting them take more of his weight. He stretched his legs further and further until his toes gently disconnected from the perch and his wingtip feathers flexed into flight. For a moment, the message reached his human reasoning that he was actually flying, and he wobbled and fell back slightly, tapping his toes on the perch. But he pushed off gently and floated up again from the perch. Then his breast sank, sending that invisible "ball" of his center of gravity rolling forward into his neck. He flapped and lifted his head to recover, but then he was too head-high, and the "ball" sank to his belly. He lurched upwards, and the feathers on the upper surface of his wing ruffled and lost their grip on the air. He panicked and instinctively pulled his feet forward, rolled his center of gravity up toward his heart, and brought his body back level again. He flapped a few times while his feet clutched about below him until he found the perch and settled back onto his toes again.

David kept his wings out and in his wide field of view, he saw Sam's wide smile enthusiastically upturned thumbs. He let his mind drift for just a moment, musing to himself that his first flight was probably about as long as the first flight of the Wright brothers. He understood the thrill, but also the dead serious concentration it took to accomplish. He brushed aside the emotional high and steadfastly concentrated on flying better.

David kept exercising this way for half an hour, gradually gaining more and more control. He fell to the floor numerous times, and Steve always made him walk downwind and then flap his way upwind to regain the perch. David loved it. By the session's end, though, he was exhausted and could barely hold his wings up on the way back to the room.

Later, after his meal, David told Sam about his experience. After describing how he had to balance his human and avian thoughts, he summed it up: *I feel like I've woken from a long sleep, Sam. Remember how thrilled we were to climb Mt. Si as kids? We got up at two in the morning and hiked long and hard until we made it to the top at sunrise. It was so still, so timeless. I felt like I could float down from there if I jumped, like nothing was impossible. That's how it was today during the session. OMG my wings are tired now but I know it's gonna be worth the pain.*

Sam stroked his nape. "Do you feel like your human and avian sides are fighting for control?"

David dropped his beak slightly as though thinking of a response. *No, not really. I can't be sure, I guess, but I think that birds have thoughts and feelings too—just no words for them. There's emotions, mental pictures, urges that don't seem entirely human yet still completely familiar. When I used to ride my bike, I just willed it to go here or there. My mind, my body, and the bike were in harmony. This seems no different except that there's no machine. I am the bike, or rather the bird. I let the bird in me be what it was meant to be, and it obeys my wishes and we're in harmony. It sounds separate, but it's not. I don't feel any separation between will and action.*

Sam's fingers slowed as he listened and massaged deeper into David's sore shoulders. After a quiet moment he said, "It sounds amazing. I'm glad you're inspired and upbeat, despite all that's happened. It's more than just flying, isn't it? I mean now you have a whole new world, a new life to explore."

David nuzzled back against his hand, burying his beak inside Sam's palm. He slowly turned back and typed: *Exactly.*

And I want to experience it with you. Thank you for being there for me my whole life. I love you, Sam. He turned his head and licked Sam's fingers.

Sam moved closer and slipped his hands under David's wings, careful not to bend his growing feathers. He touched David's skin and held him close, gently laying the side of his head down against David's beak. His eyes were moist and he whispered back, "You know it, buddy. I'm glad to hear you say that. I love you too and I'll always be right here with ya."

Chapter 13
Conflict of Interest

DR. DENNIS DUNMEIER STROKED THE fine stubble on his angular chin. He sweated under his suit jacket, and it wasn't because the conference room was hot. There were six other doctors and experts around the table, and three more on the conference phone at the center. Doctor Dunmeier looked down at his hands on the desk while all were waiting silently for him to answer a simple question: *Is David ready to go home?*

Dennis was never a natural with politics. He was a decent teacher, which was great for communicating with patients and investors. He could bring complex molecular biological concepts down to earth for those with only a rudimentary understanding and convince them to support his cutting edge research. It was easy in those cases to get what he wanted. And among his research colleagues, he was used to calling the shots, almost without question. But he wasn't used to the level of scrutiny his current situation demanded. It had been years since he had been a position to diplomatically balance a committee of egos to get what he wanted, and he knew his control of the case were slipping away.

On one hand, David was obviously ready to take care of himself. With some modification of a home environment, regular physical therapy sessions, and some appointments at the hospital, he should be able to go home and adapt to his new life. On the other hand, there would be unpredictable ramifications if the public learned of David's transformation. So far, they had managed to keep a tight lid on any credible stories leaking to the press or the Internet.

But, Dr. Dunmeier couldn't bring himself to release David from his oversight and, more important, into the public eye. His reputation was at stake, and so much more. In addition to his hospital duties, he was also medical director for the genomic laboratory of Cascadia Research Inc., the company responsible for developing David's treatment protocol. Ultimately, since he was in charge of both the creation and delivery of the treatment, he was responsible for the accident that resulted in David's transformation. Sure, he had cured David's cancer, but everyone was forgetting about that miracle. Now, it was all about David turning into a bird, and because it was an accident, albeit a happy one, Dr. Dunmeier received no adulation for it.

He chuckled often when he thought about David. It was termed an error, but what a stupendous error! It was a leap forward for gene therapy, and opened up all kinds of new possibilities, as well as lucrative opportunities. If word leaked out too widely or too soon, it could mire them in inquiries and legal battles, and delay their ground-breaking and profitable research for years. It wouldn't matter whether or not David pressed charges, Dr. Dunmeier would undoubtedly face a difficult legal exploration, which would adversely affect his credentials and research funding. He and the hospital's lawyers were already stalling for time while they tried to find a smooth and legal way to deal with the inevitable fallout.

Another facet was that Dr. Dunmeier was not only stalling for time with the hospital team, but also with Cascadia. Ever since David's amazing recovery, their demands for progress reports and budget clarifications had stopped, and were replaced with cordial requests for updates on his success. His mind flashed back to that late night when he examined the vial on his desk. His surprise hadn't been just about the labeling. His real surprise had been that David survived the initial stages of treatment. There were others at Cascadia that wanted to rush more aggressively toward the extremes of genomic therapy, and wouldn't mind seeing Dennis take the blame, fall from grace, and vacate his desirable position. Taking the blame for an accident was far less damning than being directly accused of intentionally conducting untried research on human subjects. But, he had no proof of sabotage yet.

So, until he could find that proof, and perhaps manipulate the politics of the situation more in his favor, Dr. Dunmeier had to convince the care committee's members, most of whom were as smart as he, that there were legitimate reasons to hold David longer. Fortunately, he was smarter than them in the finer points of genetic science.

He cleared his throat and said, "I need more time to be certain that David won't revert. We saw it in a few animal test subjects."

Katherine, the team pulmonologist, responded, "Wouldn't there be some warning of trouble though? He would be living with his friend less than forty minutes away."

Dr. Dunmeier put his right hand in his pocket to play with his pen, but he caught himself. It would be an obvious tell that he was nervous. He was a terrible poker player.

He stared her down and replied, "Remember the night his diaphragm and lungs ruptured? You were called at four in the morning? May I remind everyone that we didn't see that coming. What if he starts to revert and he needs immediate attention like that?" He looked around the uneasy room as people lifted their hands from the table and leaned back in their chairs with a collective squeak.

Dr. Dunmeier continued with a softer tone, "He's been here less than two months. My God! It's such a radical change. I don't think it's too much to ask for him to stay here another few weeks."

Katherine nodded. "Okay, doctor, you're ultimately the primary physician, and it's your decision. But I think I speak for at least a few of us when I say he needs more freedom. We need to figure out how to provide that. And I'd like to see some guidelines on how you'll know when we can relax about fear of genetic reversion. The facts, or at least some inferences from your animal studies. Can you have that for us in a week?"

Dr. Dunmeier replied, "Two weeks."

Katherine nodded, "Okay, you have two weeks."

Dr. Dunmeier nodded his head and relaxed inside. He knew that with a few well-timed excuses, two weeks could stretch to four. He could breathe a little easier for at least a month. That would be plenty of time to do what he needed to do. Plenty of time to solve his dilemma. Plenty of time to finish what he had begun and spin events in his favor.

Dr. Dunmeier and his research colleagues had worked for years toward the goal of using their treatments for curing incurable diseases. When the alternative was certain death, their treatments provided at least a glimmer of hope. In this current program they focused on patients with a low likelihood for long-term survival. Any good they could do, without causing harm, was seen as a benefit. But secretly they had also dreamed of testing out more radical protocols on human patients—treatments involving the use of avian or other animal DNA to destroy herpes, cure liver cancer, or even make enhancements to people. Perhaps even new species, tailor made for special purposes.

But dreaming and doing are two separate things and Dennis knew he had not crossed that ethical line of his own volition. Whoever forced his hand was brilliant and good at covering their tracks, as Dennis had been unable to find a flaw in the chain of custody for the biologics used on David. It all pointed to himself. When David presented for treatment, he was as good as dead, so there would have been fewer questions if the protocol didn't work. But now, although it worked, Dennis couldn't take full credit without also taking full liability for any mistakes.

The groundbreaking data collected—non-condemnable on ethical grounds since the experiment appeared to be human error— would be used to modulate future protocols and trials. Unfortunately, unless Dennis could exonerate himself and turn the growing tide against his professional image, he wouldn't be conducting those amazing experiments. Instead, he would be shut out and forced to watch his competing colleagues reap the accolades and financial rewards.

David's existence was as much an obstacle as an asset to Dennis' research. The only difference to Dennis was how much blame he would soak instead of his other colleagues, particularly if David were released and his story reached the public. He had to figure out how to remove the obstacle without losing the asset and, hopefully, rebuild his credibility in the process.

Chapter 14
Testing the Limits

DAVID MADE SMOOTH PROGRESS ON his flight practice. Within two weeks of starting his workouts in the basement hallway, his feathers had grown in completely, and he could deftly fly from perch to perch and all the way up and down the hallway. But his strength and speed were exceeding the confined space for no sooner would he achieve ideal flight speed when suddenly it was time to brake and land. And without vertical space, he couldn't flare his wings, tilt up, and dissipate his forward speed like an eagle normally would. He wanted to fly outdoors where he could press his performance, bank and turn, and learn to use air currents. In David's mind, he was ready to be set loose.

Despite Steve's glowing reports of David's flight progress, the medical team's official stance was still to keep David inside at the hospital. His repeated blood tests and scans showed no remaining cancer, and he was taking care of himself for the most part. Dr. Dunmeier and other team members spent less and less time directly with David, so he had to wonder, *If I can care for myself, and I'm no longer an object of constant curiosity, why am I stuck here?*

Dr. Dunmeier explained to David and Sam about his concern over genetic reversion. He also said that the medical Team wanted him to practice more flying in a larger indoor space, where he would be safe. So, a basketball court on the medical campus was outfitted for more challenging flight training, and it was decided that David would meet some benchmarks there before being released outdoors.

On David's first trip to this new location, Steve and Sam wheeled him on his cart perch down to the basement service entrance. From there he hopped onto a perch in a windowless van and was driven to the gymnasium, Sam riding along with him. He couldn't speak intelligibly but Sam noted how David's eyes scanned the dim surroundings and his wings drooped. He looked at Sam with a cocked head and questions in his eyes.

"This is weird, isn't it? Keeping you in the dark, literally," Sam said. "I'm sure you were looking forward to seeing more of the outside world than you've seen for the past six weeks in your room."

David nodded and let out a plaintive chirp.

Sam shifted and scratched his head. "Yeah, I dunno what the big deal is. Their delays and avoidance of the issue are starting to give me the creeps."

Just then, the van stopped and reversed slowly through a large door into a gymnasium. The outside doors closed with a click before Steve opened the back of the van, and David and Sam were allowed to hop out.

The gym was spacious and brightly lit. There were horizontal bar perches made of plastic pipe wrapped in rope. Some were on stands a few feet off the floor, and others hung down from the ceiling on ropes. For the moment, David ignored feeling like a prisoner and studied his new playground. He ambled over and hopped up to a perch as the others watched.

Sam turned to Steve. "Why all the secrecy and security?"

Steve exhaled and tightened his lips. "Your Dr. Dunmeier insisted. They were really specific. It seems weird to me, too, but I had to go along with it. I guess they're worried about media or someone trying to steal David. He's pretty important to them."

Sam turned and walked along with Steve by his side. "Hmm. When does that kind of paranoia stop, I wonder? When will they just back out of our lives? Sure would be nice to be done with all of this."

"I don't know, man. They don't tell me doodly. But, you know that whatever they do tell me, I'll pass along to you. That's probably why they don't tell me anything."

David looked up at a perch dangling ten meters above the floor. He swayed his head back and forth, flashing slightly offset images on his visual cortex, the part of his brain involved with eyesight. The offset images created enhanced 3D perception across his more than three hundred degrees of visual field. The fovea of each eye, a region on the retina of enhanced visual acuity, were larger and he had two per eye, unlike humans that have only a small one in the center of each retina. He could see minute details and texture, and determine distance down to the centimeter. He used all this information to ensure his first vertical flight would be a successful one.

David lifted off and pumped his wings hard, but it turned out that he was flying harder than he needed. He clutched the perch but his excessive speed made him swing forward with the perch. He wasn't prepared, lost his balance, and fell backward while still gripping the trapeze. After swinging for a moment, he dangled there, high above the floor, his wings fanned out as he hung down. He twisted his head around at his friends and chirped out his concern. The choices were clear—get back on the perch or fall to a pad that had been placed below. He wasn't sure that he had enough space below to regain flight before hitting the floor. Padded or not, the dismount would be less than graceful. Besides, there would be no pads in nature—just branches and ground. He needed to master this.

"You can do this buddy," urged Sam. He had his arms open, ready to catch his friend if he should fall. David knew it was a silly gesture. His thirty-three pound eagle body would clobber Sam if he fell on him. David flapped and tried to swing over to the top of the perch, but it wobbled and swayed like a trapeze creating equal counter-reactions that kept him in his embarrassing predicament. Then he set his sights on a sawhorse perch at the opposite end of the court. That should do! He spread his wings and flapped a few times to work up his courage and test his ability to twist upright. He flapped hard and let go with one foot, spun upright, and released his other foot. He fell fifteen feet, but poured on the power until he had sufficient speed to glide, flare, and land solidly on his target.

Steve clapped his hands. "Congratulations! You've just kicked ass on a lesson that many young eagles learn much less gracefully. That was my own contribution to this torture chamber. It was meant to simulate a thin branch on a tree."

David looked up at him, panting from the effort and eyes wide with amazement that he had succeeded.

Steve went on, "I think that the real thing will actually be easier since there are usually other branches to fall back to if you have trouble."

Sam walked over and petted David's back affectionately. "Good work, buddy. You had me fooled. You made it look easy!"

As David rested a minute, Sam pressed Steve again, close enough for David to hear the conversation this time. "Okay, so the team doesn't tell you much. Any guesses on what's up with them? Why they're dragging their feet on letting David out? You know he's performing well; it doesn't make sense."

Steve sighed and put his hands in his pockets. "I'm not exactly sure. I've told them that David's ready, but it's not my call. Dr. Dunmeier and the hospital administrator are pretty tight-lipped about timeline and release criteria. It's frustrating all the advisory members—not just me. We've been instructed not to even discuss it, so I should probably not say anything more than that."

Sam looked down at David as he softly pet him, then he put his hand around his opposite wing in a show of support. "That's interesting. They won't tell us jack either. They're going to have to let him out of here sooner or later . . . and if they won't be straightforward about it, maybe we should start letting his story out."

Steve straightened and rocked on the heels of his sneakers. "I wouldn't do that. You remember the papers that David signed. All communication about treatment is supposed to go through their PR department."

"Yeah, but that was before they screwed everything up."

Steve said, "Look, I'm on your side. It's not me doing this. I press for answers every single time we meet." Steve tapped idly around on a tablet computer, looking at vital signs transmitted from David's necklace monitor. "The other thing they're probably hashing out is what the public reaction will be. David will be swarmed with curious reporters, fans, and nutcases for months or years. He'd be a superstar and circus sideshow freak overnight. They don't want that. I can't imagine that you do either." He looked down and picked a fluffy downy feather from his shirt front and studied it in the palm of his hand. "If I was David, I sure wouldn't want the attention. I'd want to be left alone and soar away in peace."

Sam pulled his hand away, and David roused his feathers. He turned around on the perch, looking attentively at his coaches. He wished he could participate in the conversation.

Steve dropped the downy feather and let it drift slowly to the floor as he looked at David. "I can only imagine what lengths their lawyers are going through to find a way to cover their ass and keep you here as long as possible. Once you're out of here, you're out of their control. What they may not want you to realize too soon is that you hold all the cards.

But if you aren't careful, if you violate any agreements you have, you could lose the team's support and, ultimately, your financial support too."

David looked up at Sam, his red-brown eyes stirring with a desire to speak.

Steve whispered, "But, let's forget I ever said anything." Then he shouted, "Okay, David! Ready to try again?"

David looked down at his feet. He knew he would have to wait and discuss it with Sam later when he was back at his keyboard. He sighed out his frustration and looked back up at the perches. *Back to work.*

David focused on his training and made another failed attempt to land on the trapeze perch. Finally, on the third exhausting try, he found that by dropping his legs and tilting his wings steeply into almost a hover, he slowed his forward momentum enough to keep a grip on the perch and stay upright when he touched down. With a few more attempts, he learned to straighten his legs and keep his tail and hips loose when he landed too. This way, when his body swung back and forth on the perch his tail could swing up and down and cancel out his momentum and stabilize his landing. After a while, he could land so softly that the perch barely swayed.

As David rode back to the hospital, he thought to himself: *Too much effort is counter-productive. If I work with the forces and not against them, it takes less effort and everything smooths out. I want to practice this until it's second nature. I want to be as good at flying as a bird that's done it their whole life.*

Later, in his room with Sam, he was able to have a conversation again. He typed to Sam, *I learned something today that might help us bring this whole thing to a close.*

Sam sat down with a tray of meatloaf, mashed potatoes, gravy, and green beans from the cafeteria.

David typed out: *That looks just like what I'd expect to eat in a hospital.*

Sam inhaled the aroma, "Mmm…yeah. I've never learned to cook this well on my own. I'm gonna miss these free meals. Want some?" Sam held up a spork with brown-coated potato on it.

David picked at it, the aroma awakened memories of food he used to love. But as his beak touched the starchy substance his avian instincts collided and made it unappetizing. He flicked his beak and licked the roof of his mouth, a typical eagle expression of revulsion.

Thanks, but I've lost my appetite for that stuff I guess.

"Damn, man, think of how many men wished their doc would tell them to eat nothing but undercooked meat? Do you know how lucky you are?" he snickered around his mouthful.

David chortled with a squeaky twitter—his approximation of laughter. *Yeah, good point. Sorry to change the subject, but I want to talk about getting the treatment team to listen. Maybe I need to stop cooperating and that will get their attention.*

"What, like get grumpy and eagley on their ass?"

No, no, nothing aggressive. Just stop going along with their requirements. Passive resistance. I hate to stop flying as it's my only relief of boredom now that my transformation has settled out. But nothing says that I have to let them take my blood or keep wearing this damn monitor or even eat if it came to that.

Sam set his tray down and looked at David, "I don't know about not eating. You just got your appetite back and, hey, you wanna be strong when it's time to get out. But otherwise, I'm with ya buddy. I think it's a great idea. What do you want to demand then?"

David stared past Sam for a moment, thinking. Then he typed: *There should be clear parameters and criteria for me to satisfy to get outta here.*

Sam replied, "That's my bud, always thinking like a software engineer. Come on, look at you! You're ready to go!

And this is bullshit. Don't give them any more control. Make them set a deadline."

David looked down at his feet a moment, an eaglish state of reflection. *You're right. Fuck this shit. I'll tell them I'm outta here in no more than a week. If they need more time then they need to say why. And they have to let me outside, even if there's restrictions on not flying. Being inside this long is driving me crazy.*

"And you know, we could get a lawyer. These guys have been real easy to work with until now, but you're going to need your own lawyer at some point. Trouble is, I don't know what lawyer will believe this shit unless they see you. Maybe just having a lawyer come in to see you would shake this place up."

David replied: *Well, let's see how they respond to me putting my talons down about a deadline. If they balk then we'll bring in the lawyer for a meeting like you say.*

Sam reached a hand up under David's left wing and rubbed his warm, fluffy side. "You bet, bud. We'll spring you outta this joint somehow."

Chapter 15
Protest

WHEN DAVID'S WEIGHT STOPPED DROPPING, his body's major changes were over. He stayed awake longer during the day and took on more of the daily routine of an adult eagle. He would awaken just before dawn and get sleepy at sunset, though he often stayed up extra hours reading or viewing videos on his computer. But the day after their discussion with Steve, he woke up a little earlier than usual.

He had been deep in a pleasant dream, flying free over stately trees and rocky canyons, taking in every amazing detail. For a brief moment, just before waking, he realized it was a dream and thought he was going to wake back up as a human and regret leaving that state of bliss. But as he surfaced further from the depths of sleep, he remembered he was actually a bird now and could have that magical flight.

David blinked and looked around the dimly lit room and his eyes misted with disappointment. *If only I could get out of here.*

David quietly preened while his mind raced over how to start his new strategy of non-compliance. His heart raced at the confrontation that might ensue, but he resolved, with the focus of a hunter, on carrying it through.

When a nurse visited at seven-thirty am, he was cordial and cooperative as she briefly examined him, checked his monitor leads, collected his wastes, and prepared to leave. Dr. Dunmeier had stopped visiting regularly since David's transformation had slowed, so David asked the nurse to have Dr. Dunmeier stop by for an important discussion and, a few hours later, he stopped in to see David.

"Good morning, David! How are you feeling today?"

David hopped down to his keyboard and typed out, *Feeling fine, doc. No problems.*

"Well then, what was it you wanted to speak with me about?"

David replied, *Not that I'm ungrateful for all of your help. After all, you saved my life, such as it is. But I'd really like to move on. There's a whole new life for me out there, and I'm ready for it. So when do I get out of here?*

Dr. Dunmeier sat down on a stool, wearing a positive expression. "I know, I don't blame you. Frankly, I'm excited to see you get started on your new life too. But there's still more tests we have to do, and we have to be sure you won't revert. Also, we haven't prepared a place for you to live yet. We haven't made guidelines on how to announce all of this to the public either. It's complicated!"

Don't you think I know how complicated this is? I've had to adapt to being a completely different animal! David paused a moment to let those words sting. *So when are you, or they, planning on letting me out?*

The doctor replied with a faint smile, "Well, we haven't come up with an exact date."

David replied, *Okay, do you have any criteria for my release so I can work towards it?*

"You need to have a room set up at home, some method of medical telemetry for contacting us if there's an emergency. Needless to say a local emergency room won't know what to do with you. There's handling communication with the media—"

David interrupted him. *Those aren't goals I have control*

over right now. Those are action items for the committee, and so they should have deadlines attached. If there's no goals for me then I must be ready, right?

Dr. Dunmeier's smile was gone. "No, I'm not saying that. You've been flying very well but we're not sure if you're ready, eh, for the pressure of how the world might react to you."

David blinked and sighed. He realized that he was letting himself get too upset. If he pushed too hard, he could drive the doctor away. He relaxed and softened his intense expression.

I'm sure that the team means well, and it's really nice that they've been there to help. But the changes are over. I may look like an eagle, but I'm a grown man on the inside, and I have the right to make my own decisions now. I came here voluntarily and I still have the right to leave, technically whenever I wish. If they really want to see me leave as fully prepared as possible, then they'll start working with Sam and me to set up my living space, or to coach me on media relations. They should know that. The fact that it's not already occurring is concerning me.

David decided to soften his delivery even further. He looked at Dr. Dunmeier and cocked his head slightly. He softened his eyes and flared his face feathers to curl his beak corners in a slight smile. *I know that you've done your best. The mistakes made weren't entirely your fault. To be honest, this may turn out to be the greatest gift anyone has ever been given. I not only survived cancer, but I have a whole new life to live. I've done all that you wanted, and I want to keep cooperating. But it's time to include me on these decisions, and it's time to set me free.*

David walked up to Dr. Dunmeier, his massive larger-than-life eagle body giving him a stature close to the same height as the seated doctor. The doctor leaned forward, hands on his knees, his eyes steady and his expression serious, like that of a hawk staring back. Except that David saw the widened pupils, the enlarged capillaries in the doctor's eyeballs, and the sweat glands opening and moistening his brow. Those brows lifted and curled down at the sides as the doctor smiled.

Dr. Dunmeier said politely, "I'm glad to hear you say that, David. I'm glad that things are working out well for you. And I agree with you. I'll take what you said back to the team and we'll be in touch."

David's pupils rippled as he scanned the doctor's face. Faint blotches pinkened the doctor's brown cheeks, and more tiny beads of sweat popped up on his forehead. The corners of his smile fasciculated ever so slightly. His visual acuity was superior than any polygraph. *He's lying*, David thought. *He has no intention of ever letting me go.*

David ambled back to his keyboard and asked, *When, doc?*

Doctor Dunmeier was already rising to his feet and turning for the door. "I'll let you know."

As the door closed behind the doctor, David's expectations sank into his toes. He knew that the doctor was hiding something. After a day and a half with no further response, he decided that he'd had enough.

It was around four a.m. on day thirty-eight when the nurse's station monitors suddenly blared with alarms. Two nurses were on duty and checked the infrared video feed. David was standing there in the dark, preening his feathers.

"What's he doing?" one asked.

The other shook her head slowly, "I don't know but he looks okay. Could be just a detached lead or the battery died. They're due for replacement today."

They watched for a few minutes as David carefully peeled off each adhesive biomonitor lead and dropped them at his feet. Finally he shrugged the pendant off from over his neck and head. He looked up at the camera, knowing that he had an audience by that point. After a moment he looked down at the leads and transmitter pendant. He hopped down, picked them up in his beak, walked over to his toilet in the corner of the room, and dropped them in. He topped it off by defecating into the receptacle before returning to his perch. Then he swiveled his head up and stared at the camera, beak slightly down, so that his eye ridges gave him a serious look.

The younger nurse giggled, and the older one said, "Why are you laughing? You're going to have to fish it out of there and clean it up."

The younger nurse rolled her eyes. "The fun never ends. Well, it looks like he doesn't want to wear the monitor any more. What do we do about it?"

The older nurse sat down at the console and reached for the phone. "You go in and check on bird man. I think that this qualifies as non-urgent, so I'll leave a message for Dunmeier to handle it later."

A few hours later, Dr. Dunmeier came by and watched the video recording and spoke with the nurses.

"Do you need help putting the monitor back on?" asked the younger nurse.

Dr. Dunmeier sighed, smirking. "From what I see here, he's not going to cooperate. Stand by a minute."

The doctor walked to David's room and entered. David hopped down from his perch and walked straight to his keyboard.

Dr. Dunmeier started, "A little medical mutiny, David? I thought that you were going to cooperate with us."

David typed out: *No offense, doc, but I'm tired of wearing that monitor. As far as I can tell, which isn't saying much since I don't ever get to see results, I haven't needed it for weeks. And I don't think I'll let you take any more blood either, since you haven't shown me how the extra discomfort is helping me. If you want any more cooperation from me, I need to see a plan for discharging me, with dates. And, no matter what that plan says, the final date had better be no more than two weeks from now.*

Dr. Dunmeier stiffened and tensed his jaw. "Look, David, I told you it's complicated. You can't understand all the angles involved. This is a really big deal."

Two weeks, doc. Tell the team to stop dragging their feet. You have a day to give me an answer.

The doctor wagged his head a little, "Or what?"

David simply retyped: *Two weeks.*

The doctor left, his displeasure thinly disguised.

When Sam visited later, David had him disconnect the Ethernet connections to his computer, and to the video camera in the ceiling, so that they could converse in private.

David began: *Dunmeier seemed really defensive. He's probably under a lot of pressure from superiors, legal, his funders, or who knows? And now I'm just making things worse. I kind of feel sorry for him but this is my life.*

Sam nodded, "Yeah, I think he's an alright guy. A bit creepy at times, but he saved my best friend, so that counts for something. But, ya know, everyone has their point where they'll compromise to save their own skin. God only knows what they could be cooking up. I think you're doing the right thing. Not like you're insulting him or acting ungrateful, you're just making life inconvenient for him so far."

David nuzzled up against Sam's right shoulder, and Sam rubbed his nape and the feathers over his ear openings. He melted like butter under Sam's stroking, and it helped ease his restlessness.

Days went by, and then a whole week without any reply from Dr. Dunmeier. David continued to refuse blood draws, examinations, or even to be weighed. He became more and more sullen with each passing day of what had become captivity for him. The Internet stopped working the day after his mutiny began—the day he was supposed to get a reply from Dr. Dunmeier. The official excuse from the nurses was the IT department was redoing their entire network, but David knew better.

On day forty-five, Sam went along on David's daily exercise at the gym. The exercise sessions and Sam's visits were the only breaks in his otherwise dull days. He relished every moment out of his room. He flew to each perch perfectly and even did some high speed loops around the gym, passing through each trapeze, demonstrating excellent control. Steve and Sam both praised David for his abilities and cheered him on, but they noticed he was extra quiet, and focused, the entire time.

After David rested briefly at the starting perch, Steve approached and said, "I know you're frustrated and restless, David. So, I made a new exercise for you. I call it 'jump-ups.' Maybe it'll help keep you challenged." He winked at David. "And if not, it'll make you really strong so you can bust outta here when you get the chance. I use this with my hunting hawks to get them in shape for hunting season."

The exercise was a repetition of straight vertical flights up to a high trapeze perch. This was the hardest type of flight a bird could do—starting from a standstill in no wind and lifting themselves straight up ten meters. With each successful flight up and back down to the perch, Steve tossed David a bit of meat as incentive. Food is a powerful motivator for a raptor, even one with a human conscience.

The food grabbed David's senses, focused his attention on the next task and reward, and the endorphins released from eating softened the worry gnawing like a hungry parasite at the back of his mind. Soon, however, he slipped into a deeper frame of mind and even after the meat tidbits were exhausted, David was not. He panted heavily but kept driving himself up and down, up and down, pouring his frustration into the work out. Soon, he lost count of how many repetitions he had done and yet he continued to flap up, tap the perch, flutter down, bounce off the floor, and flap back up to repeat. His wings burned, salty nasal secretions drooled from his nares, and his beak hung open. He ignored Steve's shouts to stop and acted like nobody was there—just him, the perches, and his rage. As he was launching upward yet again, he was interrupted by a long, loud whistle blast. He faltered in mid-launch and flopped down to the pads below the perch.

Steve glared. "David! Enough!"

Blood surged through David's wings and breast muscles and pounded in his head. He panted with his beak open, grunting from mental anguish and physical exhaustion. He slowly fell forward and rested on his breast, drooling on the floor.

Sam looked at Steve a little worried. Steve held him back from running up to David and said, "It's okay, just give him a minute."

After a few minutes, David slowed his breathing and closed his beak. Sam softly sat down cross-legged beside him and stroked his back. "Quite a work out, bud. I think you burned enough calories for both of us."

David looked at Sam, beak tipped up slightly to simulate a sad expression.

"I know, I know," Sam said as he hugged David close.

Steve asked, "Still no response, eh?"

Sam looked soothingly down at David and petted him slowly. "Nope."

"Damn them," Steve muttered. He walked in close and sat down next to David's left wing. He started to give it a post workout massage between his two hands and glanced at Sam to invite him to do the same with the right wing.

After a quiet moment, Steve said, "You know, it sure would suck if we couldn't get the doors open to back the van in here." Sam looked up at Steve with flat brows in an annoyed stare. Steve jerked his head slightly upward and around as if to say, *We're being watched.*

Sam nodded slightly and continued massaging David's sore wing.

Steve added, "You know, we'd have to let David walk out

in the open to get in here. It'd be a great chance to get some fresh air though. Lots and lots and loooots of fresh, fresh air. There'd be nothing around him but space, even if just for a few moments."

Sam replied very quietly, "Uh, yeah, that would be inconvenient if that happened but David would like the short walk I'm sure."

Steve said, "Those door were hard to open this afternoon— like they're jamming up. I guess I could let maintenance know. Ah, but this key they gave me seems to open a lot of doors here. Maybe I could just fix it. Maybe there's a can of oil spray in the maintenance closet next to the network routers."

Sam moved his eyebrows up and down, working through where Steve was going with the conversation.

David swiveled his head around and looked up at Steve, eyes wide. Steve went on, "Ya know, that cabinet where all the cables connect from the computers, printers . . . security cameras . . . and such."

David swiveled his face around and looked back at Sam, who was smiling a little and winked at him.

Sam said, "Well, that's convenient."

Steve replied, "Yeah, that door could get stuck any day really, so it's good that we have that worked out. And hey, Sam, tomorrow's Saturday. I was going to go fly my new peregrine on the creance outside for the first time. It'd be great if you could come along."

Sam looked up briefly, "Sure, sounds great."

Steve continued, "I named her Phoenix, inspired by David here actually. You know, rising from the ashes?"

The conversation blended off into a discussion about Steve's new falcon. Sam and David had never heard of this bird but they played along. He talked about how great she was flying and how he was excited to get her to the point, perhaps next week, of letting her fly free off the creance. Sam and Steve planned to get together at dawn the next day to watch Phoenix train and prepare her for that flight.

Back in David's room, Sam disconnected the Ethernet leads to the camera and computer again and they discussed their plan. It was decided that Sam would seek legal counsel to make sure that if David left on his own volition, they weren't going to damage their future legal position and financial assistance. David felt rather guilty about the thought of suing, but Sam was the voice of reason.

Sam said, "If your treatment had gone in the way intended, you would have either died or you'd return to being a functional person who could take care of himself and return to a paying job. You can't do that now, at least not without a lot of special equipment. And you'll probably need extra care now that wouldn't have been needed if you were a person. They must be expecting you to settle with them at some point for lifetime support."

David nodded his beak and typed, *I hate lawyers and all this crap. I just want out of here. I'm glad to be alive. They treated me well, considering. But I hope I never see a hospital again.*

"There's something else, David," Sam said as he sat down close to David's side. "You probably figured out as I did that Steve doesn't have a new peregrine. I think he wants to talk about breaking you out and maybe about setting up a place for you to live."

I think you're right. He's never mentioned a falcon before and Phoenix is a pretty obvious name.

Sam chuckled and nodded in agreement, then slipped an arm up under David's wing and across his back in a warm hug. "I've been thinking about it, buddy, and I want you to come live with me."

David swiveled his eyes to Sam and bobbed his head slightly, his huge mahogany irises rippling and his pupils widening with emotion. He turned and typed, *I've been sorta hoping you'd say that. I don't want to be alone again. I want to live my life with you, Sam.* He spread his wing out over Sam's back and pulled him into a closer hug. *I love you, Sam. I won't be a burden. You're right—these guys can pay for whatever I need, and I'll do my best to take care of myself. I'll even try to be housebroken, ha ha.*

Sam chuckled back. "Well you've seen my place—nothing that a little eagle crap wouldn't fix anyway." He leaned his head against David's fluffy neck. "I love you too, buddy."

They snuggled and chatted for a while, discussing that Sam would probably not be able to visit much over the weekend because he would be hard at work preparing David's accommodations.

That weekend dragged by with mind-numbing slowness. Sam stopped by once for a short visit to let him know how hard they'd been working to prepare a room for him. David occupied himself with his own abbreviated versions of "jump ups" between the floor and window ledge of his room. The wooden ledge of the window was quickly destroyed by his huge claws but he no longer cared to show courtesy to his captors.

Monday morning, Sam visited again and brought Jim Truskie who had a special gift. It was a smartphone with a handle attached to its back. The handle projected out at an angle from the bottom right corner—perfect for an eagle to hold. Jim opened an app on the phone and explained, "The phone will wake up when picked up. Squeeze the handle once for menus. Otherwise, it's like the speech system that Stephen Hawking used except that it recognizes your face movements to help select the words. You navigate the menus and word groups by flicking your face up, down, left, or right. To erase a word or back up in a menu, flick the phone. To erase everything, shake it. When you're done, just select the SPEAK option and it will say the words."

Jim helped David calibrate it for a few minutes and then let him give it a try. He flicked his face around for a moment and then the phone spoke out in an androgynous tone, *Thank you Jim.*

David chortled and looked at Jim with beak straight on, corners up and eyes squinted slightly to convey a smile. David flicked his head about and the phone read back, "I have my voice back!"

They went on to have a conversation about how Jim had gone on a long vacation to the Caribbean. He was enjoying retirement, but also was inspired to keep helping David. And so, he cooked up this device, and had other gadgets in the works. But he was about to spend the summer at his cabin in eastern Washington, and he wanted to leave this gift before he left town. It was a great visit, and David didn't want to dampen it by raising the topic of his issues with the hospital. When the subject of his release did come up, he simply replied, *Very soon I hope.*

Jim smiled and nodded. He said quietly, "I sure hope so. You seem ready to me. When you do, come spend time at my cabin. There's eagles around, so it must be a great place to be a bird." He looked at Sam and pursed his lips. "Say, Sam, why don't you come back to the car with me. I left an accessory in there that David's going to need."

In the elevator on the way to the garage, Jim admitted that he actually just wanted to talk to Sam privately about David's situation.

Sam said, "He's beyond ready to leave. We don't know what's going on and nobody will tell us anything anymore. It's weird but David and all of us, as you know, are under a strict gag order. Not that we really know enough to tell anyone anything anyway."

They continued the conversation all the way to Jim's car. As he slid into the driver's seat, Jim invited Sam to sit inside for a minute. With the doors closed, he told Sam, "I don't like this. It doesn't feel right. They should be scared shitless and want to cooperate with you and David in every possible way. It doesn't add up."

Sam nodded and slumped. "Yeah, I agree. But what do we do? David's already started his own protest but they don't seem to care. There's enough people at the hospital that know what's going on that it's hard to imagine they'd do anything too crazy."

Jim said, "Maybe. But this is huge. Unprecedented. Hard to know what money and power could be lurking behind all of this research. Something like this could be used in so many ways. And what does it do to a person's rights when they're not legally defined as a person anymore?"

Sam looked at Jim with shock in his eyes. "Jesus! I'd never thought about that."

Jim patted Sam's knee. "Now I'm probably just a paranoid old man, but keep on your guard. You give me a call if there's anything I can do. I'm going to send you the contact information for a good lawyer, and I'll pay the bill if it comes to that. He's the caliber that you'll need for fighting this hospital."

Sam nodded. "Thanks, Jim. You know, we may be busting David out of here in the next few days, with or without the hospital's blessings. I'm setting up things at home right now."

"Aha . . ." Jim said with a nod and a twinkle in his eye. "Well you might be needing that lawyer sooner than I thought. No matter, give him a call and get in there to see him. Let him know I sent you, and I'll make sure he gets word that it's on my dime."

Chapter 16
Falling Down

TWO MORE DAYS PASSED AND David didn't see or hear from the doctor. Only the nurses, Steve, and Sam came to see him. With Sam's help, he was able to surf the Internet again through the smartphone Jim had provided. He confirmed that Jim was right to be concerned as the legal position of humans undergoing genetic modification was uncertain. It was a new issue that had no precedents in the American justice system.

After a few more days, a fifty-something short, bald, white man in a suit came by with Dr. Dunmeier. He was introduced as William Peacham, the hospital's lawyer. He was obviously not used to birds, and while he tried to be warm and courteous, he looked like he was afraid to extend his arms away from his body and touch or be touched by anything avian. The lawyer was used to talking to people across a table, not sitting face-to-beak with a huge eagle.

"David, I'm stopping by to remind you of some of the elements of the legal release that you signed before your treatment started. Now, it doesn't waive all your legal rights, and you should seek your own attorney's advice on what those rights are. But it does state that you are to remain in the treatment facility until no less than two of the doctors and the head of research agree that you can be discharged. Further, neither you nor your friends or family, nobody, can show photos or discuss treatment methods, protocols, or other details of care without permission of the doctor, the PR director, myself, or the administrator. It's hard to predict sometimes just what people will latch on to, misunderstand, and turn into an issue. It's as much for your well-being as that of the hospital. We would rather spend our time and resources on curing cancer and releasing positive news than on dealing with negative issues with the press. That said, we are preparing statements for the press, and you will have a chance to see these before they are released. Do you understand?"

David typed back: *Yes. Will I ever get to leave here?*

Mr. Peacham shifted in his shiny black shoes and looked down at David's six-inch talons as he stammered, "Y-yes, of course."

When?

Mr. Peacham smiled and straightened his back. "Soon. When you have an approved domicile set up, proper care arranged, and the doctors are convinced you can care for yourself."

You know that I came here as a human, right? I do have rights still, don't I?

Mr. Peacham leaned back a little and drew a breath, looking up at the ceiling for a moment. It was a posture that suggested he was on the defensive but also confident in his position. He spoke slowly and carefully. "Of course, David. No one is saying you don't. But it's in your best interest to let us do everything that's right for you."

David's lie-detecting eyes saw what he feared most. They were gas lighting him. The walls closed in on him and he sensed his avian instincts swelling to the forefront. He wanted to let go and let his bird side pounce on Mr. Peacham's face and rip his eyeballs out of their sockets. He feared now, more than ever, that his future wouldn't be what he had imagined it would be. If he couldn't live his own life, he'd rather that the cancer had taken him. It was clear now that he would be at the hospital for a long time, maybe forever, and they knew that they could get away with it. He wouldn't be their pet.

The doctor and Mr. Peacham tensed as David's pupils shrank, his hackles rose, and an irrational resistance to all things human smoldered to life in his eyes. He couldn't see that this line of questioning was going to go anywhere better, so he simply typed: *You should go now. I'd like to be alone.*

David walked back to his sleeping perch, hopped up, and looked out the window at the rain clouds obscuring the setting sun. His feathers rustled and vibrated as he fought to control his violent impulses.

Peacham and Dunmeier cautiously gathered their things and quietly left the room. David saw them leave out of his peripheral vision, and once gone, he sagged his head, closed his eyes, and sighed heavily.

There was indignant rage in his mind, growing with the each loud thump of his furious heart. It was different than his human anger—sharp and tense, as though the slightest stimulus would trigger him into lethal action.

David fumed as he thought about how he had unwittingly signed away his rights when he agreed to be genetically modified. *What am I now? I'm still me, though my body is bird. But to them I'm less than human, and they can treat me like an animal!*

He slapped his foot down on his perch and drew in a deep breath through his nares and held it a moment, meditating on the conflict within himself. His human and avian rage flowed together like two swollen rivers, tearing forward in the same direction. They magnified each other's destructive potential, like wind and tide on the forefront of a sea storm. His mandibles clicked tight and his jaw muscles pulsed.

David thought, *Dunmeier probably knew all of this from the start. He knew I'd either be dead, or his guinea pig— that there was no way he could lose! There's no legal precedent for a human trapped in a nonhuman body. The courts will say I'm just a bird now.*

The perch creaked and popped as David tightened his tremoring talons around it. He opened his eyes, beak low, glaring out of the tinted window at the free world. His avian and human emotions spun around in a vortex, clawing and scrabbling with each other, whirling in more and more tightly until they collapsed into a single rage. He shouted inside: *I won't stand for this! No!*

David shrieked so loud that it could be heard beyond his walls and across the ward. He looked up at the video camera above him and before he could think, he had sprung upwards, seized it in his talons, and ripped it from the ceiling. But it was still connected by a cable, so he flapped hard, swinging around on the wire, knocking down tiles from the drop ceiling. At last there was a pop as the cable gave way and he crashed to the floor. Not done, he leapt up and swung the camera by its cable so hard that it shattered the window on impact and turned it into a crazed spiderweb of crystalline cracks.

It's safety glass! They thought of everything to imprison me here!

David shrieked defiantly and threw himself against the broken window. He raged irrationally and beat his breast and head into the crumbling safety glass. There was no way he would break through it with only a thirty pound body, but he had relinquished control to his avian mind. It was in control, thrashing his body with no remorse, no understanding of windows, over and over against the invisible barrier that kept him from freedom.

Three muscular orderlies in white coats burst into the room behind David, but he took no notice. They wore face shields, padded coats, and long leather gloves. One carried a loaded syringe on the end of a pole. The others held nets and capture poles—aluminum rods with nooses at the end for securing intractable animals.

A searing jab in David's left thigh spun him around and he was startled to see the men right behind him. He flew into a panic and jumped, knocking his head against the top of the window frame and fell, dazed, back to the window sill. The world was smeared and red through the blood-stained shards and for a moment it reminded him of the stained glass windows of the church he attended as a child. His tarsi crunched sharply against broken glass, his head sagged, and then the world tilted and rolled.

David's avian rage had burned out of control, like a house fully engulfed in flames. But he wasn't completely outside of it. He glimpsed his lovely feathers mangled and stained. With cold horror he realized that no bird would do this to itself. The sparks of his anger came from his human sense of injustice and shattered expectations, concepts that were foreign to a bird. His avian fear of confinement just fanned the embers into a destructive inferno, but it was his humanity that started the fire. Somewhere deep under that wall of flames, his humanity huddled naked and sobbing, watching as his hopes and dreams, his whole future, incinerated to ashes around him. His beak drooped, his body went limp, and his talons lost their grip. His eyes were wide and unfocused with the exhaustion of a wild animal that had been pushed too far to care about life anymore. The world faded and his he pitched backward off of the windowsill and landed in a crumpled heap of bloody feathers on the floor.

Hal Aetus

Chapter 17
Shattered

"DIED? GONE? WHAT!?" SAM'S EYES flooded with tears and his hands shook as they clutched at the table between himself and Dr. Dunmeier. His heart skipped and he couldn't swallow. It flooded in that his dearest, most precious friend, was gone. There would be no life with him beyond these walls. It was unreal, impossible. "Where's David? I need to see him. Even if he's dead. I need to see him!"

Sam and Dr. Dunmeier sat across from each other in a dimly lit conference room in the hospital.

The doctor looked down at his folded hands and said, "I'm sorry but it's just not possible. He injured himself during his seizures. Some staff were injured trying to help him. It was terrible. Because of all the potential legal issues, his body is not available until all forensics are completed. Rest assured, we will treat his remains respectfully and return his ashes to you for burial."

Sam collapsed his head in his hands and bawled bitterly. "What happened? What went wrong?"

"We won't know for sure until the autopsy and histopathology is complete, but he went berserk, bashed himself into the window of his room, tore the place apart, and then had a long seizure that we couldn't stop. He finally died from trauma, overheating, and cardiopulmonary collapse. It's possible that his avian and human nervous systems just weren't as compatible as we thought. Or there was a stroke or genetic reversion. We just don't know yet."

The doctor stood up and laid one of David's large, mottled brown tail feathers on the table and put his hand on Sam's shoulder. "I'm sorry, Sam. I am truly sorry. Come by tomorrow and we'll have his things for you to pick up."

As the doctor left, Sam picked up the feather and gently cradled it in his shaking hands as though it were the delicate wing of a butterfly. Tears blurred his vision and pattered down upon it. It was a lovely feather, two feet long, but seen like this, disconnected from his friend, it was small, fragile, and abstract. Yet it was the most precious thing to him in that moment. He tried to picture David, but his scrambled reality wouldn't allow him to bring his friend into focus. He pulled the feather close to his chest and sobbed alone.

Chapter 18
Broken Bird

DAVID AWOKE IN A NARROW concrete room. A metal door stood at one end and a high window at the other. The walls had a slick, white, rubber membrane that draped loosely down the face of the cold, gritty walls. The floor was covered in neatly raked smooth pebbles. An arch-shaped bow perch covered in rope sat near the door and a horizontal perch, up high, spanned the back wall in front of the small barred window.

David lay below the window, breast down, on a blue, vinyl-covered mattress with a towel draped over him. The room flickered in his dull eagle eyes, as though the fluorescent lights had a bad ballast. In actuality, it was his eagle vision picking up the normal, rapid electrical flickering that a human visual cortex generally ignores. He flicked his dizzy head, and his pupils wobbled back and forth. He groaned, and his lower eyelids rose up over his eyeballs. He felt sluggish and heavy, just as he had when he was sedated early during his treatment.

After several minutes, he tried to rise on his shaky legs and felt the stiff crustiness of sutures and tissue glue on the skin of his breast, wings, and feet. He slumped back down and laid his head on the mattress again, swallowing the phlegm that had built up in his choana—the slit in the roof of a bird's mouth that connects to the nasal passages. His head pounded with in tune with his quick avian pulse like a mallet striking meat on a butcher's block, and his vision was blurred.

A cage dryer on the floor blew warm air over David. At least it was soothing, so he sighed and snuggled down like he was recovering from a wicked hangover. He closed his eyes as he tried to sort out what had happened. Sure, he was in a different place, obviously built for eagles, but was he still under Dunmeier's control? The last humans he saw didn't seem like the rescuing type, so he assumed he was not somewhere better.

David drifted in and out of consciousness for an unknown period of time until he heard voices and activity in the hallway. Doors opened and closed and he heard the chirps and wing flaps of other birds in neighboring rooms. He surmised that he was in an animal ward now, apparently with other eagles. But if they were also once human or merely wild birds, he couldn't begin to tell.

Suddenly a metal hatch slid open on the door to uncover a grated window. He recognized the face of Dr. Dunmeier and David's heart raced.

David slowly lifted himself to his feet and focused on the doctor's face in the gritty bluish light.

"Hello David. Stay where you are. May I come in?"

David nodded. There was an electrical click and the door swung open. Dr. Dunmeier came in wearing thick padding, leather gloves, and a face shield. An orderly was similarly dressed and had a pole syringe in one hand.

David sagged back down on the mattress. There was no use in fighting and he couldn't talk to them. He just wanted to give up and die.

Dr. Dunmeier said, "David, I want to check your wounds and give you some medicine. Will you let us do that?"

David sighed and nodded. He laid like a limp rag while

the doctor groped and patted and prodded. He let them examine his eyes and mouth. He even let them take blood from his leg. Afterward, they laid a small, dead chicken on the floor beside his mattress.

"Thank you, David, for cooperating. You might not be hungry yet, but we'll leave this for you for later."

David's lower eyelids slowly closed over his eyes. He saw the security camera blister on the ceiling and knew they would be watching. He wasn't human to them anymore and he didn't care for anything they offered. The price would be too high. He wanted to see Sam, but that would never happen. For all he could tell, Sam and the rest of the world thought he was dead and, at that particular moment, he desired that to be true. He wished for all of his sunken dreams to end in peace and darkness.

Chapter 19
Blood Stains

THE NEXT DAY, SAM STOPPED by the hospital to gather David's personal items. He went to the nurse's station in David's ward, but they were assisting an emergency team in one of the patient bays. Sam waited at the desk for a moment with sullen, hollow eyes and a face red from crying on the way to the hospital. He clutched a small backpack in his hands. He just wanted to get this over with, so after waiting a few minutes, he quietly walked down the hall to David's room. There was caution tape across the door. Sam peered in through the narrow window in the door and saw the destroyed room. The shattered window was taped over. Below that were broken glass and bloody mats but David's computer, his perches, even his toilet were all gone. Ceiling tiles were shredded and scattered around and wires dangled to the floor. It didn't look like professional demolition—more like haphazard destruction. He tried the door but it was locked. He stepped back just as a woman called out to him.

It was Nurse April. She walked to him slowly, carrying a sheet of paper. Her forehead was creased with genuine concern.

"Hi Sam. I'm so sorry about David," April said

Sam met her eyes and clutched the bag in his hands tighter. "I know, I know. I can't . . . just can't believe it."

April handed Sam the page. "This is a property form. I have everything filled out for you. Just take it down to registration and they'll have you show ID, sign it, and get David's stuff."

"Did you see it happen?"

"Yes, I did. We all heard a scream and then a lot of bumping and crashing. The orderlies were in so fast that we didn't have a chance to get involved. But I guess they couldn't do anything. They took him out of here in a hurry."

As she spoke, Sam turned and stared blankly back into the room, wanting to see his friend perched in front of the window. Tears moistened his eyes again. "Was he alive when he left the room? Could you tell? Did he say anything? Where'd they take him from here?" Sam began to break down again and choked on a throat-punching sob.

April pulled a Kleenex from her pocket and offered it as he leaned back against the wall. As he took it and pressed it to his face, April grasped his left hand. "Mr. Grand, I'm so, so sorry. Please come here and sit down." She directed him to a set of two chairs at the end of the hallway. As they sat down she asked, "Can I get you some water?"

Sam shook his head. "No. Just tell me everything you saw of David. I just have to know how he died."

"Of course, Sam. Well, the orderlies brought him out on a gurney, covered in a white sheet. I don't think that he was alive at the point because his chest wasn't moving. They took him down to the ICU, and a while later they told us that he had passed away. The room was wrecked but then, I guess you could see that already."

"What did Dr. Dunmeier try to do to save him?"

"He wasn't here at first. In fact, he had just been here with another man in a suit. But they left, so when David had his seizure, it was the orderlies that responded first."

Sam blinked and suspicion prickled the skin of his scalp. *Every other time things had gone wrong there was a full team of doctors and nurses involved but this time it was orderlies that were there first? And who were these orderlies?* He rubbed the top of his head and then blew his nose. Perhaps she'd be willing to tell him more if he asked the right questions in the right way.

Sam asked, "So, no doc was in there until Dr. Dunmeier came back?"

"Yes. Took about five minutes."

"April, I haven't seen orderlies hanging around David's room before. It's always been nurses that showed up to help him. Can I speak with those orderlies?"

"I wish you could but they were from an outside facility. They just happened to be put on special duty that day for David only. It was some new thing—probably put into effect because, well, David was getting kind of surly. Anyway, they're not here anymore."

"I know I'm being a pest, but well, this will help bring closure for me. Where were those men from?"

April folded her arms and cocked her head as she tried to remember any clues. "I think that they were from the Cascadia's ARF, that is, their Animal Research Facility, because they wore white jumpsuits and ball caps. They dressed more like zookeepers than orderlies. They also had special animal handling equipment."

Sam looked into April's eyes. "Did that seem odd?"

April shifted now a little, wondering if she was saying too much. "I don't know. Not really. David was a huge bird, and he was getting grumpy. Don't take this the wrong way, Mr. Grand, but us nurses aren't really trained to deal with animals. We deal with cranky people sometimes, but as a general rule, our patients don't bite and scratch."

The nurse glanced down the hallway and saw the other nurses gathering at the station looking back her direction. "I think I'd better be getting back to work Mr. Grand."

Sam grasped her hand and pleaded, "Please! Just one

more minute. Tell me, did you hear David say anything?" April tried to pull her hand back but he held firm.

"No, just the scream. And like I said, they brought him out on a gurney covered in a sheet. But there was blood too."

"Blood?"

April wrinkled her brows, "Yeah. I saw him lying on the gurney in the hallway here under a clean white sheet. Then I looked into the room, saw the orderlies picking up their tools. When they were wheeling him out there was blood soaking through the sheet and dripping to the floor."

"So he was bleeding?"

April looked a bit worried now. "I'm sorry, I . . . I don't really know. I wasn't attending him, so I really can't say with certainty." She tried to pull her hand back but Sam held on.

He pulled closer now, whispering more desperately, "Please April, can you get me the video surveillance? How can I get it?"

April whispered back, "Please, don't ask me to do that. I can't."

Sam shot back, "Please April, I just want to see David's last moments. He was my best friend, my family. It would mean everything to me."

She replied, "I can't!" and stood up. Sam still wouldn't let go, so she raised her voice, "Mr. Grand, let go, please!"

Sam released her hand and sat back, his face in turmoil. "I'm sorry, April. It's just . . . I don't know what to do . . . I'm sorry." He clutched his backpack and stood.

April took a step back and looked around. She turned her back to the nurse's station, the blue light from the window behind Sam reflecting off of her sharp cheeks. She pulled a card out of her pocket and held it close to her stomach, scribbling her email on the back. As she put it in Sam's hand, she whispered, "I'll see what I can do."

Just then, a doctor and a nurse came by. They were conversing between themselves and glanced at Sam and April as they passed. April pointed at the form in Sam's hand and said, "I'm sorry, Mr. Grand, but you'll have to come back tomorrow to retrieve David's belongings. It seems that they haven't all been transferred downstairs yet. Sorry for the inconvenience."

Sam nodded. "It's okay, I'll be back. Thank you, April."

Sam found his way out, his mind whirling with what he had just learned. Could David have been alive and died later? That didn't jive with what Dunmeier had told him. Maybe it was just a miscommunication, but why didn't they try to stabilize him in his room before carting him away? If he was already dead, why were they in such a hurry?

Sam nursed a black hole of uncertainty in his stomach that consumed all of his attention. That night, as rain pattered against his bedroom window, he lay in his dark room, turning April's words over and over in his mind. He didn't sleep a wink.

The next morning, Sam called in sick to work and was back at the hospital as soon as they opened for visitors. He quietly visited the registration desk and picked up David's belongings: his laptop, the oversize keyboard, some photos and get-well cards from friends, and the adapted cellphone that Jim had given him. Sam compared it to the property sheet, and to his own mental tally of what he knew David had in his room. It was complete, but he had hoped that April would have been able to download the surveillance video. Then, he noticed there was a tiny thumb drive with the hospital's logo at the bottom of the white cardboard box.

Sam closed the box, turned, and thanked the clerk. He walked back to his car, his stomach flipping somersaults at the thought of what secrets April had risked her job to give him. He drove down the street, and went into a coffee shop before he dared fire up the computer and check out the thumb drive's contents.

David's credentials for this laptop were simple since he

always had to log into it in full view of others. He hadn't had real privacy for weeks. It wrenched Sam's heart to see the desktop background picture. It wasn't the same old familiar one that had been there for weeks, a selfie that the two had taken during a hike in the Cascades the previous summer. Instead, it was a peregrine falcon with flames around it. Sam plugged in the drive, and it took him only a few minutes to find the video clips from David's last evening. He listened to the conversation with Dunmeier and Peacham. Then saw David fly out of control and rip the camera from the ceiling. It cut off at that point, so he couldn't see the last moments. He was shocked to see David explode so violently, but also disappointed that there wasn't more. Still, he could see why David would have been angry after that conversation.

Sam watched it all again and again, picking apart every detail he could. David did not seem to be having seizures, or to be delirious. He was certainly not himself, but there was intent, focus, and coordination in his actions.

Sam watched it again, this time rolling back a little farther. When Dunmeier and Peacham entered, David had been listening to music. He stopped the music with his keyboard, but he also hit another key combination. He did it casually, but Sam wondered what it was for.

Sam tried the key combination, but nothing changed on the screen. He was about to dismiss it as a failed hunch, but then he noticed that the laptop's fan kicked on, indicating that it was processing a lot of information. An error message opened, and it read, "VidWorm: Network Connection Error. Cannot access cloud account."

Sam realized that he hadn't connected to the Wi-Fi in the coffee shop. He took care of that and clicked the *OK* button. He looked at the task bar at the bottom of the window and noticed a discreet, red, circular icon that reminded him of a video record button on a camera. The LED indicator next to the laptop's camera didn't illuminate, but maybe David had disabled that. He always hated that the hospital was recording him constantly, and with his eroded trust lately, he could have set this laptop up to secretly record things that were important to him. Sam clicked on the icon, and it opened a video application. When he clicked a button to open the recording folder, he found that it was empty. He noticed that the folder was dated only a few days before, probably the day that the app was set up.

Sam said aloud to himself, "So, David had just set this up over the weekend. He was probably afraid to tell me about it since we rarely had privacy. Crafty bird."

In the settings, a 'Record to cloud' option was turned on too, as well as other advanced options Sam didn't fully understand. He tried to connect to the cloud server, and was confronted with a log in process. The email address filled in automatically but David had made sure that the password was not automatically populated.

Sam thought about it a moment. It had to be something that he knew Sam would know, but what? He tried a few words, but was concerned he might lock himself out of the account. Then he remembered the desktop background. He thought about why he would choose a cheesy picture of a falcon surrounded by flames.

Sam's eyes lit up, and he murmured, "Oh my god . . . Steve's imaginary falcon . . ."

Sam typed in "Phoenix," and the login was successful. There were only a few files including one very large final file. "Gosh they'd shut down his Internet access. He must've used the phone Jim gave him as a hotspot!"

Sam opened the last file and watched David's meltdown. He saw David rip the camera from the ceiling and rage against the window. Then, there was a jab from one of the orderlies, and he slowly collapsed and fell to the floor. He was still breathing and moving sluggishly when they picked him up and laid him on the gurney. The orderlies did not appear

to be injured, and they did all of their work smoothly, quietly, in a quick, rehearsed fashion.

Sam heard the door shut and Dr. Dunmeier's voice said,
*Good work, fellas. I guess we didn't have to go with our original
plan after all. His breathing is still too obvious, so let's give him
another dose.*

The gurney was so close to the laptop that Sam could
only see the backsides and lower torsos of the orderlies as
they stooped over David. Between the bodies, David's feath-
ered chest slowly rose and fell as he slept.

Dunmeier spoke again: *There we are. We want him to look
dead."* David's breathing slowed, became spasmodic, then
stopped. Dunmeier said, "Good! Okay, let's go! Hurry!"
They wheeled David away and the video continued on of an
empty room. Sam fast forwarded through another hour of
video to find that eventually a male nurse came in and closed
the laptop and the video ended.

Sam sat back in horror for a few stunned minutes, digesting what he had seen. *David's probably alive! But where
is he? Is he being treated well? Is he in danger? How will I ever
get him back?* He let out a long sigh, and he smiled as hope
warmed his face.

Sam spoke out loud, "He's alive!" He closed the laptop
and wiped his moist eyes. "Sons-a-bitches! Gag order be
damned, I'm goin' public!"

Chapter 20
Bob

DAVID SAT IN THE HIGH perch of his narrow cell watching the gray sky brighten outside. Light summer rain tickled the window. He wanted to open it and smell the cool morning air, but vertical wooden slats prevented access. The window looked out at a concrete wall some fifty feet beyond. It was a nothing special, but it was all he had now to connect him to the real world. He leaned forward, lifted his tail, and let fly his first dropping of the day. He no longer had a toilet to trouble with and could just go whenever, wherever he pleased. To his captors, he was just a bird now. At least the mess would also occupy the keeper longer which was David's only human contact lately.

David's plumage was full and shiny. In the dim bluish light from outside, his feathers took on the shades of a black and white photograph. His clear eyes riveted on the drops of rain hitting the puddles on the asphalt outside. His dark irises rippled and stirred, and his nictitating membranes periodically flashed across his eyes. He sat motionless except for his slow breathing and the tiny movements in his eyes. On the inside, his thoughts boiled and spun like thermals on a summer day.

David thought about whether he would ever get out of the facility alive. He thought about Sam, and what he was or wasn't told. He relished thoughts of gouging out Dr. Dunmeier's eyes and crapping in the sockets. And amidst all that, he still dared to calculate how he might one day make his escape. The pattering raindrops helped him to concentrate and cycle from one mental theme to another, passing the slow hours until he heard the click and buzz of automatic relays, and the lights of his chamber flickered on. Soon, keepers would be along to tend to him and the others.

David had had no access to computers or technology of any kind since being imprisoned in this place. From uniforms, he learned that it was part of Cascadia's research facility and he pieced together from conversations of the keepers that as far as they knew, he and the other birds were all ordinary avian test subjects, not that he had ever been a person.

By the daily tally scratches he kept by the edge of his high perch, it had been 13 days. For the first few days, he refused to eat. But, then the keepers netted him and forced food down his throat. They threatened to keep doing this if he didn't eat something every day. David decided to comply for a few reasons. First, he didn't want the goons to force him to eat. Second, he wanted to lull them into false confidence. Third, he wanted to keep himself strong and fit, ready for whatever escape opportunity may come. It was crushingly difficult at times, but he tried hard to maintain hope that he would regain his freedom eventually.

Soon there were noises in the hallway and David listened carefully to every metallic click, every squeak, every footfall, and every grunt, groan, or word spoken. His keen avian senses were sharpened all the more since he had nothing here to distract him. He used everything but his excellent eyesight to tell what was going on outside his closed door.

David turned around to face the doorway. There was a keeper that tended to shuffle his feet in short strides as he moved along. David wondered if he had hip or leg problems. For the first five days of his captivity, the man only peeked in through a grated window on the door, so David didn't know his name, but had decided to call him "Scrape." For those first days, David's cleaning was left to the burly orderlies in their protective gear, at least until they decided he was cooperating enough to let others do the work.

When Scrape finally entered the chamber, David noticed he wore a tag on his breast with the name "Bob" inscribed on it. He was an old, thin gentleman with high cheekbones hung with soft, baggy flesh that sagged around his eyes and mouth. It gave him a look of kind gentleness. He was not one of the orderlies that had manhandled David. They were large men with no physical impediments. Bob was disarming, warm, and humane, and David immediately liked him.

Bob shuffled along each morning, peeking into each cell while talking to the birds inside. He spoke like he was talking to his children. Then he opened their doors, went inside and picked up food scraps, continuing to converse with them or humming a tune the whole time. Then he scrubbed whatever was dirty, hosed down the gravel, raked, and left the room. As soon as he left each room, he rang a bell and dropped food down a chute to the floor by the door. Inevitably, David would hear birds in the other chambers immediately flutter down and scatter gravel as they seized the dead prey eagerly. Bob would usually make a comment like "Good girl, good girl! Enjoy your breakfast, pretty girl."

By listening to Bob and the chatter on his two-way radio, David learned that the cells were actually called mews. He suspected that this was a falconry term, like so many unfamiliar terms he had learned since turning into an eagle.

David cooperated with Bob because he was the only potential friend he had. He had to be an old near-retiree just trying to make a living and there didn't seem to be an unkind intention of any sort. His friendliness and non-threatening air made David hope that one day he could figure out how to communicate with him. Ironically, David's avian sensibilities that were put most at ease by Bob's gentle mannerisms while his human mind struggled to trust anyone anymore.

Bob arrived at David's door and spoke as he peered inside, "Hi there, big beautiful boy. Stay on your perch there, here I come."

The door lock clicked as Bob pressed his RF ID fob to the sensor and swung the door open. After he entered, he flipped a latch on the door jamb, so that the door stayed propped open slightly, even as an automatic closer tried to shut it.

Bob looked up at David with a smile. "Hiya big boy! How are you today?" He made some clicking sounds with his tongue, in an effort to soothe the animals he cared for.

David dropped his wings slightly and stood tall with his head feathers fluffed. He chirped as affirmatively as he could manage.

Bob replied, "Oh, good! Very nice. Such a bright boy you are. I'm just gonna clean up your scraps here first."

David watched Bob carefully, reviewing his routine. It was basically the same every day—pick up bits of prey remains, check the perches for wear and tear, hose the dirty areas of the walls and gravel, rake a bit, and leave. The only thing that varied the routine was the placement of David's droppings, pellets, or prey debris. David was amazed at Bob's level of trust. David could easily have pounced and killed Bob, yet the man would routinely turn his back on him and cheerfully whistle a tune while he worked. He occasionally glanced at David from the corner of his eye, something that he seemed to do deliberately and carefully to avoid direct eye contact while keeping track of David's actions.

David would not have been so brave if the tables were turned. He surmised that this trust probably came from working with birds for so long that he could confidently read their intentions.

Bob was a very observant fellow, and David's mind raced with thoughts of how he might communicate with him.

Without his assistive technology, it would be difficult. Also, there were cameras in the room, and he didn't want to make any communication obvious to those who might be watching.

As Bob finished up, he looked up at David and rubbed his own scalp. "I don't know what they did to you, but you are huge and handsome! You know it too, don't ya?"

David played along, he puffed out his chest, propped his wings out, and gazed out to the horizon like an eagle on a silver dollar.

Bob's eyes widened and sparkled. He gave a little clap and praised David, "Wow! You did that right on cue. Amazing! What a smart bird."

David looked down at Bob from the corner of his eye and thought: *You have no idea.* Then he resumed his normal pose and lifted his left foot to his chest then swung it out toward Bob.

Bob's mouth opened a little and his eyes furrowed. David repeated this motion. Bob was old but sharp. He had never seen an eagle do such a deliberate motion while staring him down. He replied, "You want to come with me? Or you want to come down?"

David nodded his head and Bob dropped his hose and stepped back a little. His furrowed eyebrows spasmed and his head wobbled with wonderment. "You understanding me?"

David nodded his head again.

Bob lifted his eyebrows. "I . . . I don't believe it . . ." He stepped back to the door to give David plenty of room. "By all means, come down, big fella."

David spread his mighty wings slowly, trying not to scare Bob. He flapped in place a moment then fluttered down as unimposing as he could and landed on a perch five feet in front of Bob.

The old keeper still lurched back and thumped against

the steel door. Trapped between an enormous, apparently sapient, predator and an awkward inward-opening door, Bob prepared for his potential escape by slowly raising a shaky hand to the door knob.

David saw this and remembered how Bob had alleviated his fears. He pulled his wings in, slicked his feathers down, turned his body a little and looked down at the floor to avoid direct eye contact.

Bob slowly relaxed his grasp on the knob but continued to breathe heavily. He straightened up and moved his hands to his sides. "W-Well big fella. You're even lovelier up close."

David turned his back toward Bob and hopped down to the gravel floor at the back of the room. *I have to figure out a way to lead his questions since I can only gesture yes or no.* He tried to trace a letter in the gravel while Bob looked on curiously. But the dark and cryptic color of the rocks made it difficult to follow. Bob shuffled forward two steps and peered over David's shoulders, his thick eyebrows scrunching together in concentration. David traced out a letter "A."

Bob raised a hand to his mouth and inhaled sharply. "You can write? Oh my god! What are you?"

David stopped and looked at him, his pupils pulsating and his beak tipped upwards in an effort to show a frown. His emotions churned, and he wanted to scream from frustration. *If only I could just speak!* He hung his head, dropped his wings out, and walked a few steps away trying his best to show sadness. Then he abruptly turned and looked back up at Bob. He raised his right foot and swung it up and around, then pointed at his chest. He clenched his toes into a fist and struck the rocks. Bob's eyebrows were still furrowed together in confusion, so David pointed at Bob and then at himself and then back at Bob again. *I'm human like you!*

Bob's eyebrows wobbled. "You and I . . . You and I are friends?"

David nodded his head slowly and he puffed his chest

with accomplishment. *Close enough!*

Then David had another idea. He walked over to the white rubber wall at the back of the room and he slowly traced out invisible letters with his beak tip.

Bob stepped closer and said each letter aloud as it was traced. "B, R, I, N, G . . . BRING. Oh my god. Bring what?"

David continued, and Bob recited, "P, A, P, E, R . . . PAPER! P, E, N, C, I, L . . . PENCIL!"

Just then another bird screeched in one of the nearby mews. Bob stood up straight and cocked his head toward the sound in the hallway. "Hey, big fella. You just wait a bit. I have to finish my rounds, but I'll bring something back to write on."

An hour later, Bob returned with a notebook and a pencil. He said, "I'm back, smart boy. I can't wait to see what you have to say."

David was on the bow perch waiting eagerly. He hopped to the floor and moved to the back wall, under the window. There was one wide-angle surveillance camera directly overhead in a back corner. He realized that if he drew on the wall under this camera, the viewing angle would be too shallow to see the shapes he was making. He only had to convey a short message and then hope that Bob would follow through.

Bob let the door shut completely this time leaving them alone except for the camera. David gestured with his head, and Bob complied by shuffling over close to him. He bent down and laid the notebook and pencil down on the ground in front of David. David shook his head "no" and grasped the pencil in his beak to hold it up toward Bob.

Bob's expressive eyebrows lifted and separated. "Oh! You want me to write something down."

David dropped the pencil, nodded energetically, and turned his beak to the wall to start tracing letters. Bob caught on immediately.

David scribed out slowly: "DONT SPEAK LETTERS."

Bob paused and looked at David. "Okay. Why?"

David resumed: "DONT TELL ANYONE." After a pause he added, "THEY WATCH."

Bob nodded and mumbled, "I know" as his eyes gestured up at the camera.

David continued, "MY NAME DAVID IM HUMAN." Bob repeated it under his breath. "How in the hell . . . ?" David went on, "CALL SAM 2535553113 HE EXPLAIN."

Bob's hands were shaking as he wrote the message. This was a big deal. He felt the hairs stand up on the back of his head. He glanced at the camera. This could be a lot trouble.

David traced: "PLEASE HELP."

Bob looked into David's eyes, searching for signs of humanity. He whispered, "Is this a trick?"

David shook his head.

"No, it can't be! I've worked with birds of prey my whole life, and there's no way you could teach an eagle to do this."

David chirped affirmatively and stepped closer. Bob did not shy away, but held out his hand toward David's face. David reached forward and pushed his head under Bob's hand. He hadn't had a warm touch in weeks. Bob curled his fingers under David's nape feathers and gently rubbed. David let out a low cheeping sound and blinked his eyes until tears dripped down. It took effort, but when his emotions were intense, he could still cry. He chirped softly and looked back up at Bob with his eyes and nares wet.

Bob turned his soft hand over and rubbed under David's beak. He mumbled low, "Aww, you poor thing. I'd better go before I'm missed." He whispered, "I'll call your friend."

Chapter 21
Crackpot

SAM TRIED FOR THREE WEEKS to convince any news reporter, journalist, or cop that his story was true. But he had so little to offer them in terms of evidence. And because of healthcare privacy regulations and the added fact they do proprietary research, Tukwila Cancer Center was not obligated or even legally allowed to respond to inquisitive reporters. Worse still, their public relations director, Stephanie Reed, was as smooth and capable as they come. She responded quickly to every query about David, and she never directly accused Sam of being crazy. She was warm and sympathetic when she discussed his concerns knowing full well that she may actually be recorded and, hence, speaking directly to a courtroom or the public. It left the impression that she had nothing to hide and that Sam's accusations of a conspiracy to stage David's death were baseless.

Amazingly, Ms. Reed even released some of the details of David's radical therapy and admitted that it had produced unexpected results. She mentioned feathers and "bird-like" characteristics, but didn't go so far as to validate Sam's fantastic descriptions of his friend transforming into a huge bird.

When Sam posted facts online about David's treatment and disappearance, initial responses were promising, but ultimately, the discussion was overwhelmed by the arguments of armchair commentators and Internet trolls. Experts in medicine and molecular biology weighed in and crushed Sam with soundly-written counter arguments. Conspiracy theorists eagerly fed on Sam's posts, selected out the portions that supported their skewed paranoia, and vomited it back under anonymous accounts into 4chan and other crypts of the Internet where bottom-feeders with short attention spans lurked. When he posted his hardest evidence, the video of David's final moments, a popularly trusted YouTuber discredited the footage as a hoax.

Religious fanatics jumped into the fray too and railed against medical science violating the sanctity of life and altering the Holy Order of Creation. They offered no solace, only promises that judgment would come upon the secular world because of its desecration of God's order. Religion-bashing followed, and the discussions devolved into flaming banter. Social justice warriors fumed against corporate greed and their efforts to grind humanity under their wheels of profit. Conservatives argued back, and somewhere in the chaos, most people grew weary and didn't know what to believe.

The real victim, though, was David. Everyone in the media and online were only interested in forwarding their opinion or squelching Sam's. Almost no one offered credible concern for David's well-being or his rights as a human. Instead, they bemoaned the cruel treatment of a captive bird. Some claimed that instead of transforming a person or creating a hoax video, the Cancer Center had actually cloned a Haast's eagle, an enormous eagle of New Zealand that had gone extinct 500 years before. Try as Sam might, David ultimately became faceless, dehumanized fodder for the wheels of public opinion.

Sam noted how the most vocal commentators were uncannily polarized and fast to respond. It was as if the responses were engineered. Indeed, in many cases the user accounts associated with them were recently created and shared ambiguous background details. He couldn't help but wonder if Ms. Reed and Tukwila were contracting with public image firms that used artificial intelligence or sweatshops of social media grifters to spin the story faster than the facts could be revealed.

Sam was a lone, demoralized, tired man fighting a battle he could not win. His life and career were suffering. He couldn't continue on his own. He needed expert help too.

Nearly four months after David's treatment began, Sam sat in the lobby of an upscale Seattle law firm. He had shaved that morning and wore his best white shirt, black sport jacket, and blue tie. His primping couldn't hide the dark bags under his eyes or the burdened slump in his posture. His gaunt cheeks belied he hadn't been eating well. Any more than a casual survey, and anyone could tell that he was barely holding himself together.

He had been up many nights responding to social media that continually wandered off-topic or denounced him as a fake. He had finally decided to stop trying to manage that flood of negativity. The Internet had a life of its own, and for his health he had to duck out of the way. But a phone call had changed everything.

It came at 9:35 that morning and woke him out of a fitful sleep. He was on his living room couch, still dressed, amidst crumpled fast food wrappers and an old blanket.

"Hello?" asked Sam in a sleepy, gravelly voice.

A soft elderly voice answered back, "Hi. Sam? Is this Sam?"

"Yeah. Who's this?"

The old man cleared his throat and said, "Um, my name's Bob. I can't talk long. This is gonna sound strange, but an eagle told me to call you."

Sam sat up on his couch and his laptop tumbled to the floor. "David?" he asked excitedly.

"Sweet Jesus. You know him!"

Sam levitated to his feet, ready to run out the door. "David's alive? Oh my God, David's alive? David's ALIVE! How is he? Where is he?"

"He's alive. He's a huge eagle. He's fine, but seems lonely. I had no idea . . . he just started writing things on the wall. Oh my god . . . what have they done?"

"Where are you?"

"Look, I can't stay on the phone. I need to get back to work. I'll call you back." There was a click followed by silence.

"Bob? Are you there? Bob!" He was gone, but Sam had his number on his phone and wrote it down on a scrap of paper for extra safe keeping. It was precious to him; it was a singular, feeble connection to his friend.

For the first time in weeks, Sam's heart soared with hope and it made him laugh and then cry with joy. Then the tears turned to heart-breaking sadness as he though of his friend alone and hopeless somewhere. As he sagged back into the old couch he sobbed, "Poor David. What are those assholes doing to him?"

Eventually, Sam managed to pull himself together and make some calls. Soon, he was on his way to fetch that professional help he had silently pledged. But it wasn't the grief counselor that the hospital recommended. He went straight to Bruce Fontaine, the lawyer that Jim had recommended.

Sam had already contacted Bruce three weeks prior, immediately after discovering David's video recording. They discussed that with the releases David had signed, there was little recourse but to challenge them with a suit, which would be very difficult to win without solid evidence. He also agreed with Jim that the issue of human rights would be difficult, and momentous, to defend. Essentially, David had signed permission for the treatment, regardless of outcome, and when that led to his transformation into something nonhuman, he lost his human rights as well, at least in the dispassionate eyes of the law. The sticky point would be interpreting the "intent" of his treatment. Was incorporation of nonhuman DNA fully disclosed, and was he warned of what that would mean to his rights? If not, and if David could be positively identified, then perhaps there would be a case. Bruce had needed time for research, and he recommended that Sam attempt to gather any information that might help prove that David was still alive.

Soon, Sam was in Bruce's wood-paneled office sipping a cup of coffee and watching the gulls and boat traffic of Elliot Bay. The office was decorated with Northwest Coast tribal art and carvings, as well as colorful contemporary prints. There were also framed photos of local icons, such as Mt. Rainier and Deception Pass. Sam blinked his tired eyes, trying to focus on one of the photos when Bruce came in, shook his hand, and introduced his assistant, Sue. Bruce had a smooth, tan complexion and dark eyes. His short dark hair gave way to gray sideburns and a prominent chin and jawline. Sam was sure that Bruce was Native American, and wondered if he were from a local tribe.

Sam told Bruce about Bob's call. Bruce listened carefully until Sam was done. Then he asked, "Bob didn't tell you where he was or who he worked for, did he?"

"No. He seemed pretty nervous like he was afraid of getting in trouble," said Sam.

"Did you check where the call originated from?"

Sam pulled out his cell phone. "Yeah, sure. It said Sumner, WA."

"It's local, then. We can use a service to get the precise location of that call." He turned to his assistant. "Can you go check that out? Here's Sam's number . . ." He handed her a form with Sam's contact information on it.

Sam went on to tell Bruce about his dead end with finding anyone in social media that would step forward with more leads.

"This is big, Sam. Bob may be exactly what we need," said

Bruce. "His testimony could lend the credibility and direction to get an honest-to-goodness investigation going. And if he'll testify, then we could have our day in court or the negotiating table."

In a few minutes, the assistant came back with a tablet and showed them both the location where the call originated from. A satellite image showed a compound of buildings south of Sumner. It was surrounded by forest and had only one road approaching—all the appearance of a place that would not welcome the public.

There was no map label for the labyrinthine facility, so Bruce zoomed in to the highway where the facility's driveway intersected. He opened a street view image and panned around to look at a large sign by the driveway. It read "Cascadia Research" and under that "Private Facility – No Admittance."

Bruce massaged his chin and inhaled through his nose. "So far, so good . . . looks like this guy led us to David's whereabouts."

Sam choked back tears. "Those sons-a-bitches!"

Bruce said to his assistant, "Thanks, Sue. Can you get Mr. Grand a cup of water?" He turned to Sam. "Hang in there, Sam. When Bob calls back, you need to be clear-headed and ask him some specific questions. It's moving beyond just David. Bob's job and maybe his life could be at risk. If they were willing to stage one man's death, who knows how far they could go."

Sam sniffled and sipped on the glass of water.

Bruce set the tablet down, leaned forward, and made eye contact with Sam. "Ask Bob if he's willing to meet with us. We can go to a public or private place—whatever he prefers. Ask him if he thinks that David's in danger. If he is, then we have to move quickly to get him out of there. That won't be easy. I've dealt with some cases involving corporate property, and it takes a lot to convince a judge to order a freeze and disclosure of research. And, yes, animals count as property so long as they are kept in compliance with laws for humane treatment—something that is easily whitewashed through inspection audits. I'm not trying to discourage you, especially before we have all the facts from Bob, but, well . . . just try to find out as much as you can about how Bob thinks that the facility will react. We can't lose him as our 'inside man,' and we don't want to raise suspicion such that they move David, or, well . . ." Bruce stopped.

Sam nodded and finished the sentence. ". . . Or kill him for real."

Bruce nodded.

Sam moved his eyes to the window as his mind raced through ways to get David out of there as safely and quickly as possible. "What if . . . we were to act on our own and—"

Bruce shook his head. "I can't encourage anything illegal, of course. But, hypothetically, if someone were to help David escape then I would aggressively defend them. It would require, though, that David be in his right mind and able to communicate and participate in his own defense. In other words, I'd have to be convinced that David was in imminent danger—something that would also require some sort of documentation be produced that would support his testimony. Hypothetically speaking, of course."

Sam leaned back in his seat, nodding his head. "Well, he's an excellent flyer, and a resilient soul . . . and that's not hypothetical."

Chapter 22
Last Day

BOB DROVE SLOWER THAN USUAL to work the next day. He kept peeking at his mirror, watching a white pickup truck that had been following him. He took a sip of coffee as he eased up to a red light. He had wanted to pour in some whiskey that morning to soothe his pounding heart and shaking hands, but he needed a clear head today, of all days. It was nice weather for a jailbreak: low overcast with mist that could hide even the largest bird.

Bob thought about his meeting with Sam the night before. He could hardly believe all that Sam told him. If he hadn't seen David for himself, then he wouldn't have believed it. But there David was—a thirty-three pound, gigantic golden eagle with language skills and knowledge of phone numbers. Bob had seen a lot of weird things while tending to animals at Cascadia over the past thirty years, but this topped them all.

Bob started with the company long before it was even called Cascadia, when it was just a start-up, farm-based enterprise in the late 1970s. He was a young animal sciences major who loved aviculture and falconry. Cascadia's work was the brainchild of a graduate professor and one of his protégés who saw an opportunity to help small farms increase their productivity through modern, science-based management, and selective breeding of stock. The growth of intensive farming proved to be a lucrative market for Cascadia, and they soon branched into other animal science categories.

In the 80s, pharmaceutical companies and military agencies started contracting independent, animal-based research. They led the way in the 90s with genetic mapping and identification of genes that were key to health and productivity. More recently, they had begun to capitalize on the explosive expansion of gene manipulation science and its applications in human medicine and customized task-based animal engineering.

When Bob started his career, he knew everyone, he knew the animals, he saw the positive results of the research, and he liked the positive change that resulted. He especially loved their work in captive propagation, which contributed to the recovery of endangered birds. It proved to be a positive front for the public, too, who otherwise grumbled about the strange, secretive compound in the Cascade foothills.

But with each passing decade, the work had become more and more secretive. Some of this was because of changing public opinion about the welfare of animals and their use in research. Much of it was because of corporate paranoia over leakage of trade secrets and loss of their domination of new markets of science. The almighty dollar became the real mission statement. What started as open, publicly-funded research for the sake of humans, animals, and scientific discovery, had instead become a secretive, profit-orientated dungeon where only upper management knew the goals and saw the results.

Bob understood that some of the animals he cared for were sacrificed for science. It was tough for him to see it, but he knew that someone had to care for them, and he wanted to make sure it was done as compassionately as possible. He had also been able to help the company adopt methods that actually decreased their need for as many animals to be sacrificed in the course of experiments. Although he was concerned mainly for the animals, his efforts won him favor because it was ultimately cheaper and face-saving for the company if they used fewer animals.

But as the company became more compartmentalized and sterile, Bob was less and less necessary. He moved around more slowly. The young people he had trained were twice as fast and lodged far fewer "memos of animal welfare" than Bob did. From Bob's perspective, they were fine for feeding and cleaning and caring for the animals, but they were ultimately more interested in getting the work done quickly than in doing connecting with the animals. To the newer, less well-paid generation of coworkers, the job was a necessity and little more. It was something unpleasant that was best done quickly, efficiently, with as little emotional investment as possible, so that you could get home to something more positive and fulfilling. Personal pride and empathy were once integral, but that was evaporating from the professional equation at Cascadia and it made Bob glad to be retiring soon.

These thoughts played about in Bob's mind as he continued his drive. The white pickup truck was Sam's and as it turned off and parked at an empty lot next to a car dealership, Bob felt more alone and vulnerable. He drove a little slower and a thrill rose in his chest as he closed the final mile to Cascadia's driveway.

Bob turned onto the narrow paved road and climbed the hill toward the campus. He thought about how this would be the last time he came here. The lane wound uphill through a forest of lush maple and drooping hemlock trees until he came to the gate house and showed his ID. After he passed the gate house he swiped his RF fob at another gate to enter the lot and park. Then he used the fob again to walk into the employee center. There, he had to change clothes and leave all of his personal belongings in a locker. A metal detector and screening area ensured that nothing came in and nothing went out of the research compound.

After all of that, Bob still had to use his RF badge to enter each and every ward and area within the vivarium complex where the animals were kept. Every employee was tracked throughout their day, such was the degree of vigilance against entry by animal rights activists and intellectual theft by employees. As Bob went through the long routine of entry, he secretly rejoiced that it was the last time he would have to endure the ritual. His long friendship with the company would end today. He couldn't think of a better way.

Despite the strict tracking of employees, there still was a quirky sort of camaraderie, particularly among those that had been with the company for more than a few years. Like resistance cells of humanity amongst a corporate hegemony, each section of the facility had a tribal, internal culture with their own inside jokes and memes and it made the work environment tolerable. They might celebrate someone's birthday one week, a promotion the next, and then the birth or graduation of a child the next. Any occasion to bring some color and cheer into the workplace was welcomed.

Coffee breaks were a particularly strong routine among the more senior staff. Bob entered the small avian keepers' office and took to brewing the first morning's pot as routinely as ever. He was a little earlier than usual. As the pot of coffee brewed up, he started his rounds of checking security monitors that told him all the doors were secure, all the cameras were working, and ventilation systems were running. He picked up a clipboard and checked off the daily list.

The aviculture department consisted of a collection of buildings ranging from early '80s modular trailers to the newest building which were completed in the 2000s and upgraded in the mid-2010s. The trend had been to keep the most important research subjects in the most up-to-date, secure, and isolated areas. Essentially it kept them in a "bubble," isolated from the rest of the world by layers of air filtration and climate control. David was housed in one of those newer wards.

The avian keepers' offices were in a narrow, vinyl-sided, two-story modular structure surrounded by a network of netted pens. The senior caretakers' office was on the second story with a wide view of all of the pens and breeding chambers.

Bob looked out through the windows at the avian sub-facility that he had helped build. It was getting older and emptier as needs changed and more of the birds were housed in comparatively sterile interior spaces. The wood was graying and warping, the galvanized metal curling and oxidizing. The days of doing things out in the fresh air were numbered. He felt the same way—old, decayed, stale. He sipped his coffee and mused that he was about to ventilate everything, figuratively speaking.

Bob logged on to his computer at his desk and double-checked the schedule for the day. He knew that servers were quietly logging everything he accessed. He accessed a master facility resource allocation map and schedule. It showed when birds would be removed from their enclosures for research procedures, thus making it possible for Bob and the others to plan special repairs or maintenance when the spaces were empty. A few birds were coming due for medical evaluations and golden eagle GOEA-99872 would be permanently leaving in a few days. That was David.

Bob's eyes widened and he covered his mouth in horror. Usually if an animal were being transferred, there would be more details in the schedule entry. A lack of detail was more ominous because it usually meant termination.

Bob pulled out a thumb drive from his desk drawer and inserted it into the computer. Bob pulled up David's record, but didn't pause to read it. Instead, he quickly printed a PDF copy of it to the thumb drive and put it in his pocket. No sooner had the drive settled into his shirt pocket when Darlene, the other senior keeper, pushed the door open and entered the office.

"Good morning, Darlene!" Bob said.

"Hey, Bob. How's it looking today?" she asked as she picked up a brown-stained mug and poured some coffee.

"Not bad. After our usual rounds, we'll catch up all the pigeons in loft five and crate 'em for medical evaluations. Meanwhile we can set the two newbies on loft detail to do a deep cleaning. We'll have about two hours to clean and repair."

Darlene nodded and sipped her coffee. "Sounds like a plan."

Bob looked at Darlene a moment and sipped his coffee. He was going to miss working with her. His wife had parted company years ago, and his kids had lives and children of their own. He loved them dearly, but they lived hours away. And so, the birds and his coworkers were all the family he had most of the time.

Darlene leaned her rump against her desk and stroked her short dark hair while she yawned. "These gray mornings make it that much harder to wake up."

Bob gave a half nod. "Yep . . . I agree."

There was silence while the two sipped their coffee for a few moments. Bob was preoccupied with the gravity of the task he was steeling himself to do. It felt like standing on the edge of a cliff preparing to dive off into the water. He wouldn't be able to stop the momentum of his actions, and he was uncertain whether he would land safely. His feet became as heavy as cinder blocks, and his wrinkled hand felt clammy as it clutched the coffee cup. He exhaled slow and steady, and pushed himself forward one step.

Darlene looked up at him and smiled. "I'm gonna miss these scintillating conversations I have with you, old man."

Bob almost choked on his last sip of coffee and cleared his throat. "What? Who said I was leaving?"

"Silly!" She lightly slapped his left shoulder. "You're retiring next month? Remember? You're not losing it already are you?"

Bob smiled. "Oh, oh, yeah. Sorry, I was caught off guard. No, I'm sharp as a kestrel's talons!" He said as he made a claw motion with one hand.

Darlene smirked. "Okay, well better sharpen those talons a bit."

"I'll miss you too, Darlene. Been great working with you." He gave her a warm smile. "But there's malarkey yet to shovel before you're rid of me." He picked up his handheld two-way radio and tested it briefly. "I'm gonna start with Ward 9. See you at ten."

Darlene turned her back to Bob and scanned over the sticky notes plastered all over the bookshelf above her desk. She absent-mindedly replied, "Sounds good, see you then!"

As she sat down, Bob quietly lifted a dusty set of keys that hung on a loop on the wall and palmed them so they wouldn't rattle.

He went downstairs to the diet counter, gathered up the individual tubs of food for each of the birds of Ward 9, and loaded them on a cart. Diets were made in a state-of-the-art kitchen facility elsewhere on the campus and delivered early each morning. After loading up, Bob rolled his cart out the back and up a covered breezeway toward a concrete building with "Ward 9" printed on a sign by the entrance. He waved his RF badge to the door sensor, and the door latch clicked. It still worked. Not surprising. With all of the monitoring and tracking, Bob knew that security still had a human element and his discussion with David would probably go unnoticed for a couple of days.

Bob shut the door behind himself and waved his badge over another sensor to open the second door. Two-door anteroom systems were common in most of the facility to prevent accidental escapes. His heart thumped faster and his hands shook as he slowly pulled on a pair of latex food-handling gloves. He tapped on the first door and said, "Good morning, beautiful girl!" The bird inside chirped back expectantly. "How are you today?" Bob asked as he peeked inside.

Bob continued his morning routine, working his way up the left side of the hallway and then back down the right side to service all ten of the large raptor mews. David was number eight. Bob had just finished number five when a call came on his radio. It was Darlene. He ignored it. He wanted no further distractions.

She called him again, "Hey Bob, are you reading? If you are, there's a change of plans. They want you to wait on number eight until nine o'clock. Over."

Maybe security was working faster than he gave them credit for. Or, perhaps it was a new round of tests. Either way, he couldn't delay any longer. He stepped back out of mew number six and laid down his hose. He knew that they could be watching him that very moment.

"Bob? Do you read?" asked Darlene again. Bob quickly rolled his cart back down the hallway and shoved it up against the entrance door. He pulled the keys from his pocket and locked the deadbolt. He looked up at a camera housing above the door and caught his breath. *No time to waste!*

Forgetting his impediments, Bob rushed back to mew number eight. His badge worked one more time and he swung the door open wide.

David was startled by the sudden commotion.

Bob shouted, "David! There's no time! Come quickly! Come now!"

Elation shot through David's limbs as he fluttered down to the floor. Avian adrenaline hastened his reactions and his heart rocketed into high gear. Quicker than human thought, he blew past Bob and into the hallway. His head spun to survey a commotion that sounded at the end of the hallway. Two white-uniformed, burly men glared through the narrow security window in the entrance door. He could hear the rattling of keys and urgent shouting as the men pounded on the door and hollered at Bob to open the door.

"Shit! Come on! Hurry!" Bob urged as he trotted the opposite direction toward a fire escape door at the end of the corridor. David skipped along behind him as the hallway was too narrow to spread his wings. Reaching the end, Bob slammed into the handle, and the steel door flew open amidst blaring buzzers and flashing strobes. He bent down to David, and flipped the thumb drive and lanyard over his neck. "Take this and fly to Sam! Go north! That way!" he said as he pointed towards the trees. "Look for the Car Emporium. Can't miss it. He'll be there!"

David met Bob's gaze. He wished he could express his appreciation, but he had neither the time nor the facial muscles.

A loud metallic screech and shouting voices startled David, and his wings snapped halfway out. Time slowed down as his avian nervous system shot into higher gear. It was time to flee. A woosh of cool, fresh air hit his feathers through the open doorway. Behind him there was a loud crash and cursing as the orderlies forced open the door and toppled Bob's cart.

David was in avian headspace as he looked at Bob one last time and assessed him as no threat. His eyes flashed white as he blinked his nictitating membranes and spread his wings. He jumped, bounced a foot softly off Bob's back and his wings fanned out to their full twelve foot span as he cleared the doorway. His feet touched the railing for another boost, and his momentum carried him forward into open space. Behind him he felt a slap against the side of his tail feathers as one of the orderlies made a desperate swipe with a pole net. He stroked his wings once, twice, again and again, time slowly returning to normal perception as he gained speed and climbed up over the asphalt and fences. David had only one thought and that was to fly as hard and as far as he could.

Bob and the fuming orderlies watched him climb and disappear into the mist over the alder trees at the fence line. One of them shouted on the radio while the other grabbed Bob's arm and yelled at him. Bob smiled as they dragged him away, fixing his eyes on the space in the sky where David had disappeared.

Chapter 23
The Sky Calls

DAVID SAT PERCHED ON A smooth log railing on a wide, covered porch. The porch was the front of a pine log cabin on the shore of a placid, deep-blue lake. He looked out from under the eaves at the fading stars straight ahead to the west. The cool sky before him transitioned to lighter and lighter shades of blue until it met a dim gold glow behind the cabin to the east. A steep, pine-covered hill topped with vertical crags blocked the rising sun.

David never tired of the vivid banquet of colors his avian eyes feasted upon—a world of five primary colors that spanned into the ultraviolet. Whether it was cloudy or clear, he rarely missed a sunrise, especially when he was at Jim's cabin in the backcountry of Northeastern Washington State.

A nestling crow cawed in hunger somewhere down the shore of the lake. The sound reminded David of his escape, two years earlier . . .

After clearing the tops of the trees behind the research compound, David flew low over a dense forest of alder and maple. He startled a crow family and the parents burst upwards to harass him for the next mile. He was too big to worry about harm from them, but their darting and boisterous calling only added to his hurry. He flapped hard and desperate, until his breath turned ragged and his pectorals burned, fearing that at any moment someone would snatch him and pull him out of this dream and back into captivity. He brushed the tops of the trees because any higher and he would have been in the clouds.

Before long, David saw bright white flashing lights piercing the fog and he heard traffic noise on a wet highway. As he cleared the edge of the forest, a gaudy, blinking sign at a used car lot came into focus, and below it was Sam's white pickup truck. Sam stood out front, scanning the horizon with binoculars.

David screamed out a shrill cry of joy and Sam dropped his binoculars to his chest and waved his arms when he saw David gliding in.

No sooner had he stumbled to a stop in the gravel than Sam dropped down and swept him up in his warm arms. He hugged David tight and tears ran down his cheeks. "They said you were dead! But I never gave up!"

David chirped energetically and pressed his beak up against Sam's neck and under his chin.

Sam said, "I love you, David. But there's no time to waste. We gotta make tracks!" Sam lifted David off the ground and plunged him into the truck, hopped in behind him, and punched the gas. Gravel flew as they spun around and tires screeched as they sped through the lot and out onto the highway...

In the present, a barn owl glided silently by, carrying a mouse in its talons. It fluttered like a ghost into the attic of a leaning gray barn. He heard soft hisses for the next few minutes as boisterous chicks begged for their share and his mind drifted back in time again...

Those days that followed his escape were difficult. He couldn't be alone, and he couldn't sleep for several days after.

When he slept, the darkness wasn't filled with the typical eagle dreams of amazing hunts, or stormy flights, or nests full of peaceful, sated chicks. Instead he awoke from nightmares of claustrophobic white rooms, men grabbing his legs as he tried to fly away, tubes forced down his throat, and reality slipping away as he was stabbed with needles. One dream involved Sam being beaten and killed while orderlies in white uniforms broke into his house to kidnap David.

It was days before he could sleep for more than an hour at a time, and a few weeks before he could stand to be alone for more than an hour without physical panic. He was thankful to be alive and out of captivity, but it was a long time before he felt truly free again . . .

As the daylight grew stronger, David perceived fluorescing spots in the weeds around the front yard. It was rodent urine, laden with porphyrins. It's invisible to human eyes but bright as fresh yellow paint to his. A cottontail wiggled its nose as it nibbled on clover where the weeds stood taller. Again, he drifted back in time in his thoughts . . .

Cascadia Research had initially denied everything and sternly reminded Bob of his nondisclosure agreements. But Bob was beyond caring about what they could do to him. When the thumb drive's contents were revealed, the company clammed up completely. Likewise, Dr. Dunmeier and Tukwila Cancer Research Hospital also stuck to their story that David had died and Sam was hysterical, but quieted when the stolen Cascadia medical records corroborated Sam's story.

Those records showed that an enormous eagle was admitted the same day that David had supposedly died. This eagle had multiple contusions to its breast, face, and feet that required care. The source of the bird was left blank and the records were entered using Dr. Dunmeier's access codes.

The fight didn't end there, though. David and Sam demanded release of medical records from Tukwila but they refused until a court order required it. When records were released the staff were interviewed, Nurse April divulged a lot of helpful details along with images showing David's transformation step by step. Steve also shared his observations on David's development.

As David thought on these things, the sunlight spread warmly across the hills, across the lake, and a doe stepped out from behind a pine on a ridge a mile to the west. Her ears rotated back and forth, and she stepped slowly, carefully, out into the open. David's stomach churned. He was hungry, and this doe looked tasty. She was above him though and far away—not in a position where he could ever hope to surprise and take her. Then, a fawn wobbled into view and jutted its nose up between the doe's rear legs for milk. David was not a desperate bird and would not kill a mother with a fawn. Instead, he feasted on the peaceful scene, and admired her serenity as she browsed on early summer leaves and the fawn nursed.

The sun splashed onto the tops of the pines in the yard and David knew it wouldn't be long before the dew would dry. After that, thermals would start to rise—invisible bubbles of warm air that were like elevators for birds of prey. He could already see faint ripples in the air and motes of tiny insects being lifted as his mind drifted again.

The justice system worked in the end, but it wasn't smooth and it wasn't cheap. A suit was filed, and Bruce deposed expert witnesses that assessed the records and transcripts of interviews with David. DNA analyses found sequences that were in common with surgical biopsies obtained during David's initial treatment. But there was little uniquely human DNA remaining in his blood, skin, and oral tissues and deeper tissue sampling was out of the question. So, DNA alone could not definitively prove David's human origins. After all, higher animals share a vast majority of similar genes with each other—genetic baggage left over from common ancestors eons before.

In the end, David was subjected to extensive cross-examination and it was his ability to answer any questions about his life that won the argument: David was a human trapped in a bird's body. The question of how to define where human rights applied to human-animal hybrids was shoved into the forefront of public consciousness, not soon to be forgotten or resolved. But the court did resolve that Tukwila Cancer Research Hospital was responsible for David's transformation and, thus, all of his loss in income, and his medical and legal expenses. Cascadia was charged with unlawful detainment and improper record-keeping. When the specter of charges of conspiracy to commit murder surfaced, defense lawyers moved rapidly toward a financial settlement. David and Sam were awarded a healthy sum that would allow them both to live comfortable lives with well-deserved privacy.

And privacy soon became paramount to David. He had a brief moment in the spotlight when the world learned of his transformation. The public was, understandably, curious about the life and inner thoughts of a bird. There were news interviews, webcasts, and talk shows, but it was too much for him, and he soon reduced his interviews and associations to only the most serious and non-invasive scientific research.

David swiveled his gaze towards a sound inside the cabin, and he put his foot down on his perch in anticipation of Sam's approach. He fluffed out his feathers and roused vigorously. Creaking floorboards and the sound of a faucet indicated that Sam was up and making coffee. Then Bob crossed David's mind.

How lucky it was that Bob was his caretaker at Cascadia. Any other more casual observer would surely have dismissed David's initial attempts at communication. And if they had noticed, anyone concerned for their job would have looked the other way. It was Bob that most helped restore David's fragile faith in human compassion. Bob's actions reminded him that even random strangers can be looking out for your best interest.

Bob was indemnified of Cascadia's charges against him and lauded for his willingness to take risks to see the right thing done. He permanently retired from Cascadia and, with Steve's help, started a consulting business from home to stay involved in the compassionate care of captive birds. Of course, David was also a key consultant in the business and provided an invaluable avian perspective for improving the welfare of birds in captivity.

Sam opened the front door and walked across the porch and arrived behind David. His face was at the level of David's shoulders and he pushed his nose into his back feathers. David fluffed them out and let him bury his face deep. He affectionately preened Sam's hair.

Sam muttered, "How'd you sleep?"

David chirped affirmatively.

David's feathers muffled Sam's voice. "Going out for a flight?"

David chirped.

"I wish I could come along. Maybe later today we can take a flight together."

David chirped in agreement.

Sam had taken up hang-gliding and found that he really enjoyed it, particularly with David as a copilot. David would sometimes ride on Sam's back and give him signals with his feet to let him know where to steer for the most advantageous winds and updrafts. He was never wrong.

"I'll be down by the lake, seeing if I can catch another big brownie. Why couldn't you've been a bald eagle? Then you could catch us some nice fish!"

David's eyes tightened into soft almond shapes. It was the look of comfort . . . of relaxed adoration. He turned his beak sideways and laid it atop Sam's forehead. He twittered affectionately, his eyes half-closed in bliss.

Sam whispered, "It's two years today, isn't it?"

David chirped.

Sam looked up at the bright blue sky. "Can't think of a better way to celebrate than to go for a flight." He looked into David's deep, golden-brown eyes. He said, "I love you. Always will. And I'll always be here for ya."

David's eyes reflected his supreme contentment, and he fluffed his facial feathers to pull his soft beak corners up ever so slightly. It was his practiced version of a smile, and Sam smiled back.

David opened his wings and stiffened his stance. He leaped out into the air, feet down, and pumped hard with his wings. With a mighty swoosh, swoosh, swoosh, he picked up speed and glided out over the lake. As he crossed the tall grass of the near shore, a group of mallard drakes quacked in panic and took off to the south. David exited the mountain's shadow and the sun lit up his brown body and flaming golden nape feathers. He crossed the opposite shore of the narrow lake and passed over a dark rocky hillside. His wings wobbled, and he turned to his right.

Without another wingbeat, David rose on an invisible column of air, slowly spiraling around and around in an effortless climb. He loved the challenge of seeing how far he could rise without moving a feather and this morning was perfect for breaking records. He circled high into the sky until the mountains were far below him, and he could see to the ends of the earth. The sun-cast shadow of his beak slowly shifted from one side to the other as he timelessly revolved around the wide, disintegrating bubble of warm air.

At last, David's wings rocked as the thermal dissipated, so he aimed his beak toward a distant ripple in the air to the east. He was higher than he'd ever made it before without flapping. He looked down and saw his dear friend, Sam, fishing far, far below. He closed his sun-warmed eyes and glided blissfully on, without hurry, toward the golden light.

More From Hal Aetus

Be sure to check out my aetusart.com for my artwork and current writing projects, as well as current ways you can support my independent work. If you liked The Sky Calls, you may also like these two books...

COMING SOON!

Hundreds of years in the future, humanity is gone and Volatalia, a new avian nation, has arisen from the ashes to become the crowning achievement of the Avian Age. Tristan, a young barn owl, and Pepro, a bald eagle, embark on a journey to the town of Whiterock in aid of their mentor, Kor, a grizzled but kind-hearted raven blacksmith, who is commissioned to create rings for the pair bonding of King Vasili, a noble Steller's sea eagle from a distant land, to Margerit, a renowned, intelligent white-tailed sea eagle from Volatalia. They also meet, Nyx, a peregrine falcon, and Perry, a broken-hearted Laysan albatross. The small band's simple mission becomes dreadfully complicated as they are ripped apart by forces that seek to thwart, at any cost, the joining of the two bird nations.

FOLLOW ALONG AT AETUSART.COM/WHITEROCK

Available Now!

Phil Adler wants to play professional football and live a peaceful life with his family. But a closely-guarded family secret, an ability to shape-shift into birds at will, is revealed by a rival family, threatening his hard-won career and the safety of his loved-ones. His attackers have dark, furry secrets of their own and bloody ambitions that will affect the destiny of the world. Ultimately Phil, with teamwork from his closest confidants and a few unlikely allies, must battle for his life and the survival of humankind. Written for those that fantasize about turning into a bird and taking to the skies, The Adler Chronicles draws you into a family of werebirds who quietly live among us. See how they live, love, care for the natural world, and fight for their existence.

AETUSART.COM/THE-ADLER-CHRONICLES